JOHNSON COUNTY PUBLIC LIBRARY
3 2938 00459 3748

W9-CKH-242

THE IRON GATES

Also by Margaret Millar in Large Print:

Spider Webs

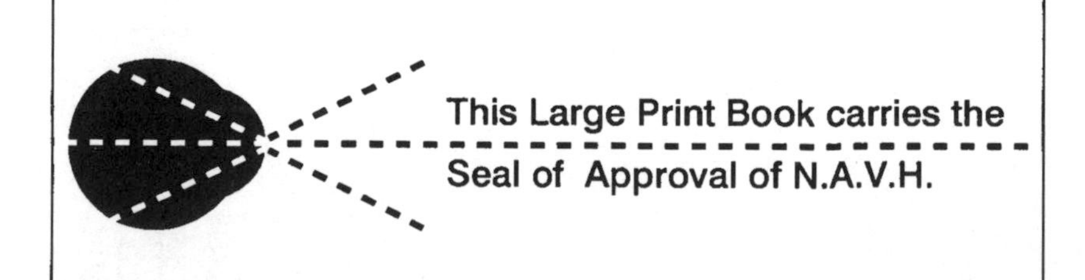

THE IRON GATES

Margaret Millar

Thorndike Press • Thorndike, Maine

Published in 1999 by arrangement with
Harold Ober Associates, Inc.

Thorndike Large Print® Mystery Series.

The tree indicium is a trademark of Thorndike Press.

The text of this Large Print edition is unabridged.
Other aspects of the book may vary from the original edition.

Set in 16 pt. Plantin by Al Chase.

Printed in the United States on permanent paper.

Library of Congress Cataloging in Publication Data

Millar, Margaret.
The iron gates / Margaret Millar.
p. cm.
ISBN 0-7862-1779-0 (lg. print : hc : alk. paper)
1. Large type books. I. Title.
[PS3563.I3725I76 1999]
813'.54—dc21 98-51091

To Frances MacNaughton

CONTENTS

PART ONE

The Hunt

CHAPTER 1

The dream began quietly. She and Mildred were in a room and Mildred was curled up in a chair, writing.

"What are you writing, Mildred?" Lucille said. "You are writing, what are you writing?"

Slowly, dreamily, Mildred smiled, "Nothing, I have finished, I have quite finished," and she rose and walked through the window into the snow.

"You mustn't go out just in your dress like that, Mildred, you'll catch cold."

"No . . . I'm going away. . . . I'm quite finished. . . ."

"No, it's dark, it's snowing."

But she walked away inexorably, leaving no tracks, casting no shadow.

"Mildred, come back! The back of your head is open!"

"No . . ."

"You're bleeding. You'll make the park untidy."

"I'm going away," Mildred called back, softly. "Good-bye, dear. Good-bye, Lucille."

She walked on, between the trees, and up and over the hills. With each step she became smaller and smaller, yet more and more distinct, as if neither time nor space had the power to blur her details. Now and then she turned around and she was always smiling, like a little doll.

"Little doll!" Lucille cried. "Little doll . . ."

"Away," came the answer, soft as a whisper but so clear. "Good-bye — good-bye, dear. . . ."

Eternally she walked and bled and smiled and grew clearer and clearer.

Lucille awoke, suffocating, sick with horror at this tiny thing moving across her mind, no bigger than a finger, a match, a pin. She sprang from her bed and pulled aside the curtains that shrouded the windows. She looked out, and there was the park, there were the trees, the hills, the trackless snow. But Mildred had been dead for sixteen years.

Somewhere in the distance a church bell rang out the Sunday sound of a city. She became suddenly conscious of how grotesque she would appear if Andrew should walk in and find her like this, crouched beside the window, scanning the snow for his dead wife.

She rose and turned, and caught sight of herself in the mirror. She had forgotten the mirror was there, and for an instant, before she had time to set her face, she seemed a stranger, a lady in a mirror, no longer young, wearing a blue nightgown, with her red-gold hair swinging against her shoulders in two long thick braids. She paused to look at the stranger, smiling faintly because it was only a game, yet uneasily because games were never just games, Andrew said, there had to be some motive behind them. Perhaps even after fifteen years that was how she still felt, like a stranger in the house, visiting someone else's husband and someone else's children.

"Oh, nonsense," she said aloud, and walked quickly toward the mirror and the stranger moved and grew and became herself. "What utter nonsense!"

Her tone was the one she used with Andrew and the children, half-severe, half-humorous, completely understanding. The I'm-smiling-but-I-mean-it voice. The sound of it was so familiar that automatically the accompanying facial pattern sprang into place. Her eyes lost the strained anxious look and became kindly and intelligent, her full firm mouth softened, onc eyebrow rose a little.

That's better. This is how I really am. This is me. Lucille Morrow.

Mildred wasn't important any more, though her portrait still hung on the living-room wall, and now and then she bobbed up in dreams. A fat kewpie doll carved out of soap, Lucille thought. Something doughy and sticky you couldn't get off your hands . . .

She picked up a brush and began to brush her hair vigorously. With each stroke the dream receded and the doll blurred and melted.

Her moment of insecurity had passed and left her with a more conscious sense of possession. This was her hand, her brush, her house, her husband whistling in the adjoining room. Only the children could never belong to anyone but Mildred. For Andrew's sake Lucille had tried to like them and make them like her in return. But they remained Mildred's children and she was uneasy with them and the most she ever achieved was an armed truce.

Still, they were no longer children. Polly was getting married this week, and some day Martin would marry, and she and Andrew would be left alone in the house. With Edith, of course, but she didn't count.

Her hand paused. She gazed into the mirror and saw the future stretching out in front of her, a length of red-velvet carpet covered with a marquee.

She dressed quickly and coiled her hair in a coronet around her head. Like a queen she moved out into the hall, proudly but cautiously, as if she must test the red-velvet carpet and measure the height of the marquee. She walked down the stairs enjoying the sound of her taffeta morning coat following her with obsequious little noises like a genteel servant.

Upstairs, a door slammed and Andrew's voice shouted, "Lucille! Wait a minute, Lucille!"

She paused at the bottom of the steps.

"What is it, Andrew?"

"What's happened to my scarf?"

Lucille checked an impulse to say, "What scarf?" She said, "All your scarves are in your bureau drawer."

"All except this one and this is the one I want to wear."

"Naturally."

"What did you say?"

Lucille raised her voice. "I said, naturally, the one you want to wear is the one that isn't there."

"It's the other way around," Andrew

shouted. "The one I want to wear is the one . . ."

"All right," Lucille said, smiling. "What does it look like?"

"Blue. Dark blue with little gray things on it." He came to the head of the stairs and gesticulated. "Little gray things like this."

He was a tall, gray-haired man, nearly fifty now, but he was still slim and he had the quick vigorous movements that characterized his son Martin and his sister Edith. His features were thin, almost delicate, but he had large soft brown eyes which gave his face an oddly guileless expression and caused him trouble now and then with his women patients. Like many really good-natured men, when he tried to look cross he overdid it. He sent a ferocious scowl down the steps at his wife.

"Somebody gave it to me for Christmas last year," he said.

"I did," Lucille said serenely. "And it's not blue, it's black. Have you looked under your bed?"

"Yes."

"Andrew, why? Why do you always look under beds for things first?"

"It's the logical place. So much room. Lucille, you wouldn't come up and . . ."

"I wouldn't," Lucille said. "If I came up

and found it for you it would only make you crosser."

"I promise."

"No." She turned calmly and walked away, flinging over her shoulder, "Try the cedar closet in the hall."

Ignoring Andrew's noises of distress she went into the dining room.

Edith and Polly were already at breakfast. Edith was buttering a piece of toast with the precise contemptuous movements of one who despises food as a necessary evil to be gotten over with as quickly as possible. Polly, a cup of coffee in front of her, was smoking and gazing dreamily out of the window.

"Good morning, Edith," Lucille said. She bent over Edith's chair and the cheeks of the two women touched briefly. It was a routine of long standing. They were fond of each other, in a dry expedient way, for they were of the same age and they were interested in the same thing, Andrew. "Good morning, Polly."

"Morning," Polly said without taking her eyes from the window.

"Good morning," Edith said. "Sleep well?"

"Fine."

"More than I did." Her voice was so high

and sharp that it seemed ready to break into hysteria, or snap with a death twang like a violin string. Every year it seemed to Lucille that Edith's voice got higher, that the string was pulled more and more taut and played a thin sinister obbligato over the most ordinary remarks.

"What is all the shouting about?" Edith said. "If you want fresh toast, ring for Annie. I told her to have it ready. Sometimes I think Andrew likes to shout simply for the sake of shouting."

Lucille sat down, smiling, and unfolded her napkin. "Perhaps."

"I've seen him at the office simply oozing quiet charm, and when he gets home he howls, he does, he really *howls.*"

"He couldn't find a scarf he wanted," Lucille said.

She felt suddenly and absurdly happy. She wanted to laugh out loud, she felt the laughter forming in her throat and she had to force it down. She couldn't explain to Edith or Polly that she wanted to laugh because this room was warm and bright, because it had begun to snow outside, because Andrew couldn't find something and had looked under the bed. . . .

She looked at Edith and Polly and for a minute she loved them both utterly, because she was so pleased with herself and the beautiful quiet life she had built out of nothing. *I love you, my dears, my dears. I can afford to love you because I have everything I want and neither of you can take anything away from me.*

"Andrew never could find anything," Edith said. "And the closer it is to him, of course, the more trouble he has finding it. I suppose it's psychological."

Polly stirred slightly. "What is?" she said. "No, don't tell me. . . ."

"Finding things," Edith said. "I expect Freud would say that you find only the things you really want to find. Some people have the most wonderful gift for finding money. There's a man in New York . . . Polly, it would be *nice* if you sat up *straight.*"

"What for?" Polly said.

"You look as if you have curvature of the spine all huddled up like that."

"I'm not huddled, I'm relaxed."

"The table is no place to relax."

"O.K.," Polly said without resentment, and uncoiled herself from the chair. For a minute she remained upright, and then she propped her elbows on the table and supported her head in her hands. Her long black hair swung silkily over her wrists.

"Honestly," said Edith, in affectionate exasperation.

Lucille remained quiet. She no longer made any attempts to discipline her stepchildren, and even when she was especially annoyed with one of them she had enough self-control to refrain from comment. She had always tried to be fair to them and when they disagreed with their father she often forced herself to take their side against him. But in spite of her efforts they had remained aloof and careful.

Perhaps it's because they were at a difficult age when I married Andrew, Lucille thought. Polly was only ten, and Martin twelve, and they were both so fond of Mildred.

Mildred, Lucille thought, and found that the laughter in her throat had evaporated like the bubbles in a stale drink.

"Though I never relax myself," Edith said, sitting very upright, "I don't mind others relaxing in the proper place. It depends on the personality whether you can or can't."

"Mildred," Lucille said, "Mildred had a very relaxed personality."

She hadn't said the name aloud for years, she didn't want to say it now, but she forced the words out. Her moment of complete happiness had gone, and it was as if the warm bright room had led her on and deceived her and she must cast a corpse into it for revenge.

"Yes, she had," Edith said shortly. "Though I think you should have enough sense not to . . ."

"Yes, I know," Lucille said in confusion, conscious of Polly's hard steady stare. "I'm very sorry."

"Today of all days," Edith said.

"I'm sorry, Edith."

"I'm glad you are. Today of all days we don't want to be reminded of unpleasant things. We must make a good impression on Mr. Frome."

"Lieutenant Frome," Polly said. "And you needn't bother about the impression. I made that weeks ago."

"Still, we *are* your family, my dear."

"He's not marrying you."

Edith blushed and said sharply, "I realize that he's not marrying me and that no one ever has, if that's what you're getting at."

"Please!" Polly said, and got up and planted a quick kiss on her aunt's cheek. "I didn't mean that, silly. I meant I hate fusses, and so does Giles. I don't want this to be a today-of-all-days. Giles'd curl up and die if he thought he was putting anyonc out by coming here."

"Then he's too sensitive," Edith said crossly.

"I know he is. That's why I'm glad he's got me. I'm not." She put her arm around her aunt's shoulders and whispered in her ear, "It's lucky I'm not sensitive or how could I have stood all your crabbing?"

"Crabbing?" Edith's mouth fell open. "Really, Polly! As if I'd ever stoop to crabbing!"

"You do crab," Polly said, laughing. "And you make speeches."

"Well, I never! The nerve of . . ."

"Confess it, confess it now or I'll tickle you."

"Oh! You sit down right this minute and behave yourself." Edith smoothed her ruffled hair and feelings. "You and your jokes. You're worse than Martin. As if I ever made speeches. Do I, Lucille?"

"Never," Lucille said, with a smile.

"You see, Polly?"

But as soon as Lucille was brought into the conversation Polly's mood changed. Her face became a blank, her eyes fixed themselves coldly on Lucille and Lucille read in them: "See how nicely we get along without you? This is how you've been spoiling things for us all these years."

"I don't believe in making speeches," Edith said. "I think the tongue is a much overrated organ."

"Isn't it," Polly said absently, and strolled over to the window, her square shoulders outlined in the light.

Lucille glanced at her and was struck again by the difference between Polly and the rest of the family. There was something compact and uncompromising and stubborn about even the way she was built. She was rather short, and though slim, she gave the impression of sturdiness and durability. She did not expend her energy haphazardly and aimlessly like Martin and Edith. She moved with a kind of lazy competence and she did nearly everything well, and was at home anywhere.

Her features had the soft roundness of her mother's, and she was, like her, fundamentally a tranquil person. But where Mildred's tranquillity had been deepened by happiness and security, Polly's had been warped and hardened by years of implacable hatred of her stepmother.

Perhaps with Martin alone I would have been successful, Lucille thought. He's a man, and more pliant. But Polly . . . Polly seemed already grown-up at ten. She distrusted me, as a grown woman distrusts another woman whose house she has to share.

Edith had finished her coffee and her long thin fingers drummed restlessly on the tablecloth. She had finished one thing, breakfast, therefore she must start another thing at once. Whether the activity was her own or someone else's did not matter. She was constantly on the move and setting other people in motion.

"I wish Andrew would hurry," she said. "I expect Martin to be late, of course. I think I'd better go up and see what's keeping them."

"Lots of time," Polly said. "Giles' furlough doesn't begin officially until noon and it won't take us over an hour to drive out to the camp."

"I understand," Lucille said, rather shyly, "that officers have 'leaves' and enlisted men have 'furloughs.' "

Polly shrugged, and said, without turning around, "Oh, do you?"

"I think I — I heard it somewhere."

"Really?"

"Of course, so did I," Edith said hurriedly. "Though I prefer to call it 'furlough.' It sounds so much more important, Polly. Why Andrew and Martin insist on driving out with you I don't know."

"They want to look him over first," Polly

said, "and then if he doesn't measure up they can dispose of the body some place and bring me on home, teary but intact."

Edith tried to look shocked. "I'm sure such an idea never entered Andrew's head."

"I was joking, darling."

"What a way to joke!"

"But the main idea, I suppose, is to give Giles the impression of male solidarity behind me. 'None of your funny work, Frome, or else . . .' 'Be good to our little Polly' — that sort of thing."

"I consider it quite touching," Edith said.

"Yes, isn't it? And so redundant. They both know that since I have decided on Giles, nothing in this world can stop me from marrying him." She glanced briefly at Lucille.

"I'm glad you feel like that," Lucille said quietly. "It's bad policy to interfere with marriages."

The girl flushed and turned away again.

"There's altogether too much fuss made about marrying," Edith said. "When I was young I naturally had some experience with moonlight and roses, but the roses nearly all turned out to be the crepe-paper ones from the dime store, and the moonlight no better than a street lamp, not so good for seeing purposes." She smiled affectionately at

Polly's back. "But I expect you've known that for years."

"Off and on," Polly said. "I lapse. This is my nicest lapse."

"I'm really very anxious to see him," Edith said with a break in her voice. "It's so hard to believe you're old enough to be getting married. It seems like yesterday . . ."

"I never thought you'd get sentimental about me."

"As if I'd ever get sentimental," Edith said and briskly pushed back her chair. "I'm going up to hurry Andrew along. If he looks for the scarf much longer he'll have the whole house torn up."

She went out in a flutter of silk and sachet.

Left alone with her stepmother Polly came back to the table and poured herself another cup of coffee.

Because she felt embarrassed with Lucille she focused her eyes carefully on the objects on the table, examining and appraising them as if she were at an auction — the silver coffee urn with the little gas flame under it, the red cups on white saucers, the remains of Edith's breakfast, two pieces of toast sagging against the toast rack, a bald and imperturbable boiled egg in a red bowl, and a corner of Lucille's blue sleeve.

"I'm glad Giles could get his — his furlough," Lucille said politely.

Polly did not look up. "So am I, naturally."

"Three weeks, is it?"

"Yes."

"And you're being married on Friday — five more days."

"We have to wait for the license. Then we'll go down to the registry office and get the mumbo-jumbo over with and be off."

"Where are you going?"

Polly shrugged. "Here or there. It doesn't matter."

"No, I guess not," Lucille said, and the two were silent again.

In the hall there were sounds of laughter and running footsteps, and a few seconds later Martin came bursting into the room. His hair was rumpled and his tie wasn't tied but he had the self-assurance and smiling arrogance of a man who has achieved success early and easily. He had had his back broken when he was a child and sometimes his walk was stiff and painful; but he never talked about it and he was almost always smiling, and if he lived a secret bitter life of his own behind the smile he never let on.

He looked so much like his father that Lucille's lips curved involuntarily when she saw him and her eyes were soft as a lover's.

"Edith just flung me down the stairs," Martin said cheerfully. "What in hell's the hurry? It's only nine-thirty and the Big Four don't meet until noon."

He pulled out a chair and sat down, and ran his two hands over his hair to smooth it. In the process he knocked over a cup on the table and narrowly missed Polly's head with his elbow.

"I don't think Giles is going to like you, Martin," Polly said crisply. "You're too violent."

"Of course Giles will like me. I'm going to give him lots of advice. I'll tell him everything a young man in his condition should know."

"He's twenty-nine, darling. A year older than you are."

"But totally lacking in experience."

Polly made a face at him.

So far Martin hadn't even looked at Lucille but she knew the omission was not deliberate as it would have been in Polly's case.

She did not want to call attention to herself by speaking, so she watched the two of them in silence, forgetting Mildred and taking pride in the fact that these were Andrew's children and both of them so good-looking and dark and clever. Martin was literary editor of the Toronto *Review*, and very young for his job. Polly had taken her degree in sociology at the university, and for four years had worked in various settlement houses doing everything from investigating cases to helping deliver babies.

"Is that my egg?" Martin said, pointing to the red bowl.

"Nobody can own an egg," Polly said. "They're so impersonal."

"I can."

"Don't take it," Lucille said, laughing. "It's not very warm. Annie will make you another."

But Martin had already sliced the top off the egg, and was choosing a piece of stale toast from the rack. Lucille poured his coffee for him and then rose to leave. She would have liked to stay on at the table as she usually did on Sundays, but she knew she'd be in the way. Martin and Polly were already deep in a discussion of how Martin should and should not behave to Giles.

"Do *not* be funny," Polly said. "And above all do *not* slap him on the back or ask him what his officer's swagger stick is for. Everyone asks him that and it's very embarrassing because he doesn't *know*. And above all . . ."

Lucille closed the door softly behind her.

She stood for a moment in the hall, uncertain of herself and her position, not sure what to do or where to go. She had a sudden shock of recognition.

I've been here many times before, she thought. Alone in a hall with the doors closed against me, a stranger, a tramp.

She had a vision of herself, her body bent forward in lines of furtiveness like a thief about to tiptoe past a sleeping policeman.

Then from upstairs she heard Edith's voice raised in angry solicitude, "I do believe you've given yourself a fever, Andrew!" and abruptly everything became normal again, the policeman woke, the thief was caught and put neatly behind bars, and Lucille's thoughts folded and packed themselves into their proper files.

"My dear Edith." Andrew's voice was raised too, and he sounded nervous and irritable. He doesn't want Polly to get married, Lucille thought. He still thinks of her as a little girl. "How can anyone *give* himself a fever?"

"You know very well what I meant," Edith said. "You're coming down with a cold, and it's a lot of nonsense anyway, this dashing out into the snow to meet . . ."

"My dear *Edith*. I am not dashing out into

the snow. I intend to conduct myself in a dignified manner in a *closed* car with a *heater,* providing . . ."

"You know very well . . ."

". . . providing I am allowed enough privacy to get dressed."

"All right, *get* double pneumonia."

"Dear heaven!" Andrew said, and a door slammed.

Lucille walked down the hall, thinking, with a smile, of Edith. Poor Edith, she thrives on imminent catastrophes and likes to think of herself as the great Averter of them. . . . I could do the menus and make out the shopping list for tomorrow. . . . I wonder if Giles is allergic to anything. . . .

She went into the small book-lined room that Andrew called his den. The sun hadn't reached this side of the house yet and the room was gloomy and smelled of unused books.

She turned on a lamp and sat down in Andrew's chair and stretched out her hand for a memo pad and a pencil. She began to plan the menus for the week, with one eye on rationing and the other on Annie's limitations in the kitchen. Lobster, if available, and a roasting chicken. Mushrooms, or perhaps an eggplant.

She bent over the pad, frowning. She

wanted everything to be perfect for Giles, not because he was Giles and about to marry Polly, but because she was Lucille. She had the subtle but supreme vanity that often masquerades under prettier names, devotion, unselfishness, generosity. It lay in the back of her mind, a blind, deaf and hungry little beast that must always be fed indirectly through a cord.

While she planned she drew pictures absently on the back of the memo pad. Vaguely through a sea of lobsters and shrimp she heard Edith's voice calling her.

"Lucille, where on earth are you?"

"In here. In the den."

Edith came rushing through the door with an air of challenging a high wind.

"I think Andrew's caught a cold," she said with a tragic gesture. "Today of all days. His face is quite flushed."

"Excitement," Lucille said. Edith was smoking, and her pallor, seen through a veil of smoke, reminded Lucille of oysters.

"Oysters," she said.

Edith looked a little surprised. "I loathe oysters. Unless they're covered with something and fried."

"Yes."

"I don't like the *color* of the things."

"Neither do I," Lucille said calmly, and

added oysters to the list.

"Though I wasn't, as a matter of fact, talking about oysters," Edith said with a certain coldness. "I was talking about Andrew. I think he should be sensible and stay home today."

"Oh, leave him alone, Edith." Seeing her sister-in-law's color rise she added quickly, "Andrew hates to be babied. The best thing you and I can do is to stay out of everyone's way. Leave the three of them together. In a way it's their morning, we mustn't interfere. For the present — we're — we're outsiders."

Edith looked as if she were about to continue arguing, then with a sudden twist of her shoulders she turned and sat down on the edge of the desk.

"You're so reasonable, Lucille," she said, almost complainingly. "I don't know how you do it, always putting yourself in some other person's place and coming out with exactly the right solution. It's extraordinary."

"I've had a lot of practice." Contented and smiling she leaned back and touched her hair lightly with the tips of her fingers. The little beast had been fed and had stopped gnawing for a moment.

A few minutes later Edith went out, and

Lucille sat with the memo pad on her knee, patiently waiting for Andrew to come in and say good-bye to her. But he didn't come.

He's forgotten you.

Well, of course he has. He's with his children. It's their day, after all. I said it myself.

But he *has* forgotten you.

Well, of course. I'm not a dewy-eyed bride any more. . . .

She got up and went to the window and stood waiting to catch a glimpse of him as he left the house. She saw the three of them going up the driveway, close together, arm in arm. With the snow whirling around them they seemed like a compact unit, indivisible and invulnerable.

While she watched, a squat dark cloud moved across the sun like a jealous old woman.

Lucille stood, wanting to cry out, "Andrew! Andrew, come back!" as she had cried out to Mildred in the dream.

But no sound came from her lips, and after a moment she went back to her chair and lighted a cigarette and picked up the memo pad again.

She looked down at the pictures she had drawn while she was planning the menus. They were women's faces, the faces of fat silly kewpie-doll women. They smirked and simpered at her from the paper and tossed their coy ringlets and fluttered their eye-lashes.

Detachedly, almost absently, she burned out their eyes with the end of her cigarette.

CHAPTER 2

Around noon on Sunday, December fifth, the Montreal Flier was derailed about twenty miles from Toronto. The cause of the derailment was not known but it was hinted in the first radio reports that it was the work of saboteurs, for the train had been passing a steep bank at the time and the number of people killed and wounded was very high. Volunteer doctors and nurses were asked to come to Castleton, the nearest hospital.

Edith heard the news on the radio but paid little attention to it beyond thinking fleetingly that death and catastrophe were so common these days that one had to be personally involved to get excited over them.

"All volunteer doctors and nurses report at once to Castleton Hospital, King's Highway number . . ."

She rose, yawning, and turned the radio off, just as Lucille came in.

"What was that?" Lucille asked.

"Some train wreck."

"Oh. Lunch is ready. Any calls for Andrew this morning?"

"Two." Years ago Edith had appointed herself to answer Andrew's calls on Sunday. She said wistfully, "Remember the old days when I used to spend nearly the whole day at the phone?"

"Andrew is sensible not to work so hard," Lucille said. "His assistant is perfectly capable."

"Still it was rather fun to be so busy."

"Not for Andrew." She smiled, but she was annoyed with Edith for bringing the subject up. She and Edith, between them, had made the decision that Andrew was to retire, at least partially. Now that he had, Lucille was beginning to doubt her own wisdom. Andrew's health was better but he had spells of moodiness.

"Doctors are too hard on themselves," she said, as if to convince herself. "That's why so many of them die young."

"Don't talk about dying. It upsets my digestive tract." She turned away, biting her lower lip. "It makes me think of Mildred. . . . I can't help wishing you hadn't referred to her this morning, especially in front of Polly."

"I'm really sorry. It just slipped out."

"You'll have to be careful. She might not want Giles to know how — how Mildred died."

"She's probably told him already."

"No, no, I don't think so. Such a terrible thing." Edith closed her eyes and Lucille saw that the lids were corpse-gray with the blue veins growing on them like mold.

"So bloody," Edith said. "So — *bloody.* I — really . . ."

"Edith, you mustn't." Lucille put out her hand and touched Edith's thin pallid arm. "Come along and have your lunch."

"I couldn't eat a thing."

"Certainly you can."

"No. Just remembering it upsets me. . . ."

"We'll see," Lucille said, a trifle grimly.

She walked out, leaving Edith to wander wispily behind her like a little unloved ghost.

Lucille estimated the situation and acted as usual with good sense. Given any sympathy or encouragement Edith would mope herself into indigestion or a migraine.

"Sweetbreads for lunch," Lucille said cheerfully.

Edith brightened at once. In spite of the tug of her conscience she saw Mildred floating away out of her mind and the blood frothed into yards and yards of beautiful pink gauze trailing Mildred down the years.

"I adore sweetbreads," she said.

She ate too heartily and had indigestion anyway, and by two-thirty she had begun to fidget because Andrew and the children hadn't returned. Lucille tried to calm her and succeeded only in making herself nervous and impatient.

At four o'clock Lucille built a fire in the living-room grate to cheer them up. But the wood was damp and the flames crept feebly up along the log like dying fingers beckoning for help.

"They should *be* here," Edith said. "They should *be* here. I can't think what has happened."

"Probably nothing at all," Lucille said and poked the log again and turned it.

"I told you that wood wouldn't burn."

"My dear Edith," Lucille said, "it *is* burning."

"Not really burning. I'm surprised at Andrew worrying me like this, I'm surprised at him. He should know better."

"How could Andrew know you were going to eat too much and make yourself nervous?"

"You're going too far, Lucille."

"I should have said that two hours ago."

"It carries a nasty implication," Edith said coldly. "As if I would not worry about Andrew if I hadn't eaten too much, which

I'm not admitting in the first place. I think you might. . . ."

The telephone in the hall began to ring. The two women looked at each other but did not move.

"Aren't you going to answer it, Edith? It's probably a call for Andrew."

Edith didn't hear her.

"An accident," she whispered. "I know — an accident. . . ."

"Don't be silly," Lucille said and went out to answer the phone herself.

The operator's nasal voice twanged along the wire.

"A collect call from Castleton for Mrs. Andrew Morrow. Will you accept the call?"

"This is Mrs. Morrow. Yes, I'll take it."

"Here is your party. Go ahead."

"Hello," Lucille said. "Hello?"

For a moment there was no reply but a confused background of sound. Then, "Hello, Lucille. This is Polly."

"What's happened?"

"There's been an accident."

"Polly. . . ."

"No, not ours. We sort of happened into it and Father and I are staying to help. There's a little hospital here, that's where I'm phoning from."

"Polly, you sound funny."

"Maybe I do. I've never seen a train wreck before. Anyway, I'm in a hurry. There aren't enough doctors and nurses. Tell Edith not to worry. Good-bye."

"Wait — when will you be home?"

"When they can spare us. Martin and Giles are helping get the bodies out. Good-bye."

"Good-bye," Lucille echoed.

Edith was tugging at her sleeve. "What is it?"

"Nothing much," Lucille said. "There was a train wreck and Andrew's helping."

"How awful!" Edith said, but the words meant nothing to Lucille. She was looking over Edith's shoulder, smiling. Andrew was safe, her world was safe. All the trains on earth were of no importance if Andrew wasn't on them.

She hurried back into the living room to stir up the fire. . . . Andrew would be tired when he came home, he would like a fire and a hot toddy.

But no matter how hard she worked, the wood refused to burn. She rose to her feet, dusty and defeated. Slowly she moved her head and her eyes met Mildred's. Mildred, whole and happy and done in oils, and changeless, Mildred, still a nuisance after sixteen years, having to be dusted once a day and sent away to be cleaned when her plump white shoulders showed scurf.

Lucille looked at her bitterly but Mildred's soft sweet mouth did not alter, and her blue eyes undimmed by time or tears or hate stared forever at a piece of wall.

"It's all coming back to me," Edith said.

"What?" Lucille said. "What?"

"The wreck I was trying to remember. It was when Andrew and I were practically children. I don't remember how it happened exactly but the train was derailed in some way not a mile from the house. And of course we had to go over as soon as we heard about it."

She went on and on, and Lucille heard only snatches. "Hundreds of bodies, yes, hundreds . . . very unpleasant for children . . . soldiers to help because the other war was on then. . . ."

In the excitement Edith's indigestion disappeared, and Lucille acquired a headache.

"You're becoming more moderate with the years," she said sharply. "The last time you told me, it was thousands of bodies."

"Oh, it was not," Edith said, offended. "I'm very accurate at numbers. You're not yourself today, at all, Lucille. You're quite critical."

"I have a headache."

"Go up and lie down then. You're not yourself today," she repeated.

"I don't want to lie down," Lucille said and was surprised to hear how childish she sounded.

Edith and I are not friends, she thought. We get along and laugh together and understand each other but with only a little less control we might rail at each other like fishwives.

"Very well, I'll lie down," she said. She walked abruptly to the door hoping that if she hurried she might defeat Edith by having the last word.

But she was not quick enough.

"Well, I should *think* so," Edith said.

Breathing hard, Lucille went to the staircase and began to ascend. She wanted Edith to hear how briskly and youthfully she went upstairs, but the deep carpet and her own weariness betrayed her and the sounds she made were the soft treacherous sounds of a panther moving across the uncertain floor of a jungle.

She had intended to pass the hall mirror without looking at herself but now that she had reached it she couldn't bear to turn her head away and slight an old friend.

"Hello," she said, quirking an eyebrow to show herself how whimsical she was being saying hello to herself. "Hello, stranger."

She passed down the hall into her own room.

As far as anything in the house could be free of Mildred, this room was. In Mildred's day it had been the guest room because the windows looked out over the park. Mildred had draped the windows herself with yards of suffocating ruffles and net and visitors saw the park only through a pink fog.

Lucille's first act had been to strip off the ruffles and replace them with crisp tailored drapes. There was a chair beside the windows and here Lucille often sat watching the people in the park, in the winter the skiers and the children with sleds and toboggans, in the summer the parade of prams and picnickers and cyclists.

There was one very steep hill that hardly any cyclist ever managed to get up, and Lucille found pleasure in estimating at just what point the bicycles would falter and the riders dismount and trudge up the rest of the hill.

She enjoyed the people who used the park. They were so tiny and harmless and always making things difficult for themselves by going up and down hills. But she especially loved the cyclists, the ones who never reached the top. Cruelly she enjoyed their endless and futile activity while the clock on her bureau ticked away the minutes and the years.

Outside it had stopped snowing. The park lay like a silent lolling woman softly draped in white with hints of darkness in its hollows.

Lucille turned from the window. She did not like the park at dusk. For a long time after Mildred died nobody had gone into the park after nightfall. There were rumors of a man who roamed the hills with an axe in his hand, there were tales of ghosts and half-human animals. But Mildred and the man were soon forgotten, and intrepid children and impatient lovers had driven away the ghosts.

Only Lucille remembered the man with the axe. She had never believed in him for an instant, yet some perverse part of her mind had kept him for her in storage. When she was disturbed and restless he came out from hiding, gently at first so that she would think he was an old friend. His face was smiling and familiar and she never saw the axe in his hand or the blood on his clothes until it was too late. Then gradually his face would change and distort into something so grotesque and hideous that she could never describe it in words or even remember it when she was feeling calm again.

Lucille laughed suddenly, thinking of Edith.

"Edith would say I have repressions," she said aloud. "Poor Edith."

She went to the mirror and began to make up her face for Andrew.

"If you're tired," Martin said, "why not let me drive?"

Andrew did not take his eyes off the road.

"Gravel and snow," he said. "I think I'd better keep the wheel."

Polly's voice came from the back seat, "You should know by this time, Martin, that Father thinks nobody can drive as well as he can."

"Never saw one," Andrew said.

"The trouble with you . . ." Polly said.

"The trouble with you," Andrew said, "is you talk too much, my dear. You're likely to give Giles the right impression."

"Giles," Polly said, "do I talk too much?"

The young man beside her stiffened in order to show her that he was alert and listening to her. But he hadn't heard the question at all. A combination of circumstances had made him so ill at ease that he was aware only of his own problems and discomfort.

In the first place he didn't feel quite at home yet in his officer's uniform. He didn't know what to do with his swagger stick, and though he felt that he should put his arm around Polly he didn't want to lose the stick, or break it.

He was, moreover, nervous with Polly's family. How could they talk like this after seeing the wreck and the bodies?

The wreck had affected him more than the others because he was not used to death and sickness and because it was a little bit like war and he was going to see a lot of things worse than this. The knowledge clutched his stomach like an iron hand.

He sat up straighter. In the headlights of an approaching car his face was stern and white, and the small fair moustache he was growing only emphasized his youth and helplessness.

"Forget about it, Giles," Polly said, seeing the misery in his eyes.

"Forget about what?" he said stiffly.

"Everything."

"Oh."

She squeezed his hand. "You look awfully nice in your uniform."

"Thank you."

"I'm sorry we had to run into this today, darling."

"Don't be sorry," Giles said. "I mean, it's all right. I mean, it's not your fault."

"True," Martin said dryly.

He rather liked Polly's young man, but he was in no mood to go easy on him. He himself had been stirred by the wreck to pity and anger which, in Martin, turned at once into sarcasm.

"Martin doesn't want anybody to know he's human," Polly said, "so he'll be biting and snarling for a week now."

"Like the cur I am," Martin said.

"Martin loves snarling."

"Don't you both?" Andrew said, suddenly irritated with the road and his children and their endless wrangling and the young lieutenant who wasn't good enough for Polly.

"I don't," Polly said. "I get along with everybody."

"Lack of taste," Martin said, slumping further on the seat. "Your chief fault."

More uneasy than ever, Giles cleared his throat and tried to think of something very correct to say. By the time something occurred to him Polly and Martin were talking again. Frustrated, he began to beat his stick rhythmically against his knee.

The can glided over the treacherous road. On a curve the wheels slipped and lurched ahead and the car sprawled sideways in the middle of the highway.

"Better reconsider," Martin said. "I'm a heller on snow and gravel."

"Kindly shut up, Martin," Andrew said, twisting the steering wheel furiously.

"I'm trying to save trouble," Martin said. "Lucille will blame me if I don't deliver you cosy and safe at the door."

"See?" Polly said to Giles. "Now he's biting Father. I think we should feed the poor mutt and walk him past a hydrant."

"What?" Giles said, and blushed. "Oh. I see."

Martin grinned into the darkness. "You can't blame Polly for being earthy now and then. She's had such a wide range of experience. Tell him the case of Mrs. Palienczski, Polly."

"Not until after we're married," Polly said calmly.

Married, Andrew thought, and his fingers dug into the steering wheel. Polly getting married, staking her life on the chance that this young man was clean and decent and responsible and healthy . . .

I don't like him, Andrew decided.

Once the words had formed in his head, the feeling which had been vague before became definite and irrevocable. "I don't think I like him," had become "I'm determined I'll never like him."

Andrew was not given to introspection or self-analysis — he had been too busy for it all his life — and so he thought his judgment of Giles was perfectly impartial and well-considered, and, of course, correct.

"It's nearly midnight," Martin said.

"Nearly midnight," Giles echoed, and was conscious of a feeling of relief that the day was almost over and tomorrow could be no worse.

For the rest of the journey he was silent. Every now and then when they passed a lighted village he would glance down at Polly's dark fur coat. He had never seen her wearing it before and it looked very expensive, like the car, and Martin's hat, and Andrew's watch. In addition to his other fears he began to be afraid that the Morrows were rich, that they might have servants who would intimidate him, that he wouldn't know which fork to use. Or he might slip on a waxed floor, or break an antique chair . . .

Anyway, I'm a soldier, he thought. Anyway, that's more than Martin is. I'm a lieutenant with a whole platoon of my own.

He closed his eyes and wished that he could be back where he belonged, with his platoon. . . .

"Giles," Polly said. "Darling, wake up. We're here."

He was awake immediately and reaching instinctively for his swagger stick. But his mind was confused and when the car jerked to a stop he had the impression that Andrew had driven right up on to a veranda, a spacious veranda with huge white pillars. He blinked slowly and looked out the window and saw that the car had stopped under a portico. Between the pillars he could see the din sprawling hills of the park.

"You take the car in, Martin," Andrew said wearily and climbed out of the car.

Martin slid over on the seat. "All right. Remove yourselves back there."

"Come on, Giles," Polly said. "We'll get out here."

He was still staring out the window at the park. A park he thought, their park, a whole damn park in the middle of a city.

"Come *on*," Polly said. "You can moon over the scenery some other time. I'm cold."

Giles got out. There was a brisk clumsiness in his movements as if he hadn't quite got used to his own size.

"Is it yours?" he said. "All that?"

"Of course not," Andrew said brusquely.

"Really, Giles," Polly said, laughing.

"That's High Park. We happen to live next to it. You'll love it, Giles. Tomorrow we'll walk through it. . . ."

"No, you won't," Andrew said. He turned his back to them and pressed the doorbell. He spoke over his shoulder and his voice sounded thin and distant. "I don't want to be tyrannical about this but I must insist that you stay out of the park."

"I'm afraid you've caught a cold, Father," Polly said.

"You must stay out of the park," Andrew said. "It isn't a nice place."

"Of course, sir," Giles said stiffly. "Of course, sir. I don't like parks."

"I'm afraid Father is overtired," Polly said. "Martin and I often go into the park, especially in the winter to ski."

"It isn't a nice place," Andrew said, and pressed the bell again.

Martin came running up the driveway. He had his hat off and his dark hair was feathered with snow. He threw his hat up in the air and caught it, and let out a shout that was an exultant challenge to the weather.

Giles stood, shaken with envy and wistfulness. *I'd* like to do that, he thought. I could do that.

"Martin is always uninhibited," Polly said, "but especially in the first snow of the year."

The portico light went on suddenly, and the door opened.

Giles had a confused impression that several women were rushing out at him all talking at once. . . . "We didn't hear the car. . . ." "Andrew, you didn't tie your scarf. . . ." "You're not chilled, Andrew?"

Polly's voice rose above the babble, clear and cold.

"Come on, Giles. I'll fix you a drink while they're taking Father's temperature."

The talk died down and Giles was able to see now that there were only two women. One of them was tall and thin and looked like Martin, with her dark curly hair cropped close to her head. She had bright birdlike eyes and a wide mobile mouth and it surprised Giles to hear how high and tight her voice was and how anxious her laugh. This must be Edith, Giles thought.

The other woman was taller, and seemed at the same time younger and more mature than Edith. She had the controlled subdued beauty that plain women sometimes acquire when they have achieved happiness and success and security. Her red-gold hair was coiled in a braid around her head.

She came toward Giles, holding out her hand and smiling apologetically.

"We've been terribly rude," she said.

"You're Giles, of course. I'm Lucille Morrow."

He shook her hand, very embarrassed because he still had his gloves on and because Polly had flounced ahead into the house without looking back.

"How do you do?" Giles said.

"And this is Edith, Polly's aunt. Edith dear, come over and meet Giles."

Edith darted at him. She was wearing something that fluttered in the wind and it seemed to Giles that she was entirely fluid and never stopped moving, talking, smiling, having ideas.

"Hello, Giles," she said. "What a pretty uniform, don't you think so, Lucille? We are so glad to have you here, Giles. Andrew, please go into the house at once, though you probably have pneumonia already."

"Nothing I'd like better," Andrew said and stamped ahead into the house.

"What a way to talk!" Edith slipped her hand inside Giles' arm. "Polly is always rude, don't mind her. One of the first things you have to do is teach her some manners. We've never been able to."

Giles found himself being guided expertly and firmly into the house and down a hall. He had no time to look around or even to think. Edith did not once pause for a breath or an answer.

Her hand on his arm was like a bird's claw, helpless and appealing, yet somehow grotesque. He thought if he moved his arm the claw would tighten from fear and the harder he tried to shake it off, the tighter it would cling.

"Here we are," Edith said, and thrust him neatly into the living room.

Lucille was pouring out the hot toddies. Martin and Polly were sitting on the chesterfield talking, and Andrew stood in front of the fire warming his hands.

"Attention, everybody," Edith said. "And Polly, this means you as well as everyone else because I'm going to make a speech."

"I knew it," Polly said tragically. "I knew it."

"How could you know it when I just decided myself?" Edith said. "Besides, it's a very short speech, and I consider this an occasion."

"And occasions deserve speeches," Martin added. "Preferably by Edith. Come on over here, Giles. We may be up all night."

"You will if you keep interrupting me," Edith said. "Anyway, I want to welcome you to the house, Giles. We are glad you could come and we think you will find us a

— a happy family." She blushed and gave Giles an embarrassed and apologetic smile. "I know how sentimental that sounds but I think it's true, we are a happy family. Of course we have our lapses. Polly is invariably rude and Martin's high spirits are a trial. . . ."

"And Edith gets maudlin," Polly said.

"Oh, I do not," Edith said. "And Andrew can never find anything and then he gets cross, don't you, Andrew?"

"I may become justifiably irritated," Andrew said, "but never cross."

"As for Lucille," Edith said and smiled across the room at her sister-in-law.

There was a pause and the room seemed to Giles to become static. It was no longer a real room but a picture, the man standing warming his hands at the fire, the two women smiling and smiling at each other, the three figures on the chesterfield relaxed and yet unnatural. Happy family, Giles thought. An ambitious picture painted by an amateur. The smiles of the women were set and false, and the figures on the chesterfield sprawled ungracefully like stiff-jointed dolls.

"As for Lucille," Edith said, "I don't believe she has any lapses."

Lucille laughed softly. "Don't you believe

her, Giles. I'm the worst of the lot."

His eyes met hers and he felt suddenly warm and understood and contented. The rest of the family with their constant jokes and squabbles were a puzzle to him, but he felt that he knew and liked this quiet beautiful woman.

Something stirred in her eyes like mud at the bottom of a pool.

"I haven't seen you before," she said. "Have I?"

"No," Giles said uncertainly.

"For a moment you reminded me of someone."

"There!" Edith said triumphantly. "That's Lucille's lapse. Someone is always reminding her of someone."

Lucille said, "Life is an endless procession of faces for me. I am always trying to match them up."

She picked up her glass and looked into the murky liquid. It seemed to come alive and surge with millions of little faces, winking, frowning, sly, puckered, brooding, bitter, smiling little faces, incredibly mobile and knowing. She could not close her eyes and blot them out. She knew that then they would appear behind her eyelids and that she must walk alone through this delicate soundless hell.

When Giles said good night to her she was still holding the glass, looking into it with bewildered melancholy, like a child trying to comprehend the universe.

"Good night, Mrs. Morrow," he said.

She raised her head, and in her quick nervous smile he saw a flutter of questions: You? Where do you fit in? Have you a place? Have I?

"Good night, Giles," she said in a composed voice. She glanced across at her husband. "Coming, Andrew? It's very late."

Very late, too late, later than you think . . . I mustn't let my nerves bother me like this, or I'll dream of Mildred again.

CHAPTER 3

In the late afternoon of December the sixth Lucille Morrow disappeared.

The house had been quiet all day. Martin and Andrew were working, and Edith had gone on a shopping tour with Polly and Giles.

In the kitchen the two young servants, Annie and Della, were cleaning silverware. When the front doorbell rang Annie snatched up a clean apron, tying it as she ran along the hall.

As soon as she opened the door she regretted this waste of energy. It wasn't a real caller but a dark shabby little man in a battered trench coat.

"Mrs. Morrow?" he said hoarsely.

Annie, who admired Lucille, was both flattered and angry at the mistake.

"Mrs. Morrow is resting," she said, in a voice very like Lucille's own. "She cannot be disturbed."

The little man blinked, and shifted his feet. "I got something for her. I got to give it to her. You go and get her." He turned up his coat collar and then slowly and patiently put his hands in his pockets. “Special delivery like.”

“I’ll take it,” Annie said. “And why you can’t use the back door is more than I can say.”

“Very special delivery,” the man said, but his voice lacked conviction. He seemed to have lost all interest in the matter and wasn’t even looking at Annie any more. “What the hell, you give it to her, I give it to her, what’s the odds. Here.”

He brought one hand out of his pocket, and thrust a parcel at Annie. Then he turned with a jerk and walked away, his head lowered against the wind.

Annie closed the door and looked at the parcel. It was a small rectangular box wrapped in plain white paper. Perfume, Annie thought, and shook it to see if it gurgled. But the parcel remained noncommittal and neither gurgled nor rattled.

Briskly Annie mounted the steps and knocked on Lucille’s door.

“Come in,” Lucille said. “Yes, Annie?”

“A parcel for you,” Annie said. “A funny little guy brought it.”

“Man,” Lucille said.

“A funny little man, then,” Annie said. “Don’t you think my grammar is getting swell, Mrs. Morrow? Della noticed today, I sound just like you."

"Yes," Lucille said. "You're a very clever girl."

"Oh, I'm not really clever," Annie said modestly. "I just figure, here is my chance to get cultured so I try to get cultured."

"That will be all, Annie."

"I figure, chances don't grow on trees. I could be making more in a war plant but what would I be learning, I tell Della."

Lucille waited in silence and after a time the silence penetrated into Annie's consciousness and she turned, with a small sigh, and went out.

She had barely reached the kitchen when she heard the scream. It rushed through the house like a wind and was gone.

"My goodness," Della said. "What was that?"

The two girls looked at each other uncertainly.

"I guess it was her," Annie said. "I never heard her scream before. Maybe she twisted her ankle. Maybe I better go up and see."

But when Annie went up Lucille's door was locked.

"Mrs. Morrow," Annie called. "Mrs. Morrow. You hurt yourself?"

There was no answer, but Annie thought

she heard breathing on the other side of the door.

"Hey," Annie said. "Mrs. Morrow!"

"Go away," Lucille said in a harsh whisper. "Go away. Don't bother me."

"Della and me, we figured you twisted your ankle or something. . . ."

"Go away!" Lucille screamed.

Her spirit bruised, Annie returned to the kitchen.

"Well, I like that," she told Della. "You hear her? She *yelled* at me."

"And her usually so quiet," Della said. "But then she's just at the age. Sometimes they go off like that." Della snapped her fingers.

"Who?" Annie said.

"Women," Della said mysteriously. "At that age. Hysterics and fits over nothing. Maybe she didn't like what was in the parcel. Say it was jools, emeralds, say, and she didn't like them. Say she gives them to us."

"To us," Annie breathed. "Oh, Lordy."

"A necklace, say."

The silverware was forgotten. The emeralds were sold, except two. ("We should keep one apiece," Della said.) The money was invested in war bonds ("I believe in war bonds," Annie said), and flowered chiffon dresses and mink coats ("Exactly alike," Della said. "Wouldn't that be cute?" "Except you're fatter than I am," Annie said).

The argument over a red roadster was interrupted by the ringing of the telephone.

"Red," said Annie, "is vulgar," and picked up the telephone.

"Yes, Dr. Morrow. Yes, I'll call her, Dr. Morrow."

She turned and hissed at Della, "Him. For her. You go and tell her."

"Well, I won't," Della said. "Nobody can call me vulgar and expect favors all the time."

Stubbornly, she turned her back, and Annie, seeing that nothing short of a sharp pinch would move her, decided to go herself.

When she arrived upstairs the door of Lucille's room was open and Lucille was missing. Annie called out several times, and then, in a fit of exasperation, she searched Lucille's room and the adjoining bathroom, and the room beyond that, which belonged to Andrew.

Della was called, and the two girls looked through the entire second floor, now and then calling, "Mrs. Morrow." The silence made them nervous and each time they called their voices were shriller and higher.

Clinging together they came down the stairs and switched on all the lights. The house ablaze with light no longer seemed so quiet, and Annie moved almost boldly ahead into the living room.

"Wait," Della said. "I thought I heard something. I thought I heard a — a foot-step."

"You heard no such thing," Annie said, shaken.

"Oh, I don't like this," Della moaned. "She's done away with herself. Things like that happen at her age. Oh, I wish people would hurry up and come home."

"She didn't do away with herself, we would've found the corpse."

Once the idea of death had entered their heads the girls became too frightened even to talk. Silently they went through all the rooms on the first floor.

There was no trace of Lucille Morrow or the box she had received.

The girls returned to the kitchen and the more familiar scene loosened their tongues.

"Maybe it was really emeralds," Della said, "and instead of giving them to us she's gone out to throw them away, say, or have them reset."

"How could she go out?" Annie said.

"Weren't we sitting here in these very chairs? Did anybody ever come in or go out that I don't know about, I ask you."

"We could go up again and see if any of her coats are missing."

"I don't want to."

"I was just saying we could."

Annie's curiosity was whetted. A minute later the girls were on their way upstairs again.

In the clothes closet Lucille's dresses hung, ready to be worn, and shoes lay on the racks ready to be stepped into.

"It's like looking at a dead person's things," Della whispered. "You know, after they're dead when you sort out their clothes and there they are all ready only nobody to wear them."

"Oh, shut up," said Annie, intent on studying the coats.

"I got a funny feeling, Annie."

"Oh, you and your feelings. It would serve you right if she walked in here right this minute and fired us both for getting into her things."

Dreading this possibility, and yet feeling that it would be an improvement on their present situation, they cast longing fearful glances toward the doorway.

But Lucille didn't walk through the door

and neither of the girls ever saw her again.

They returned to the kitchen and Della suddenly noticed that the telephone receiver was still dangling on its wire. Instead of merely presenting this fact to Annie, Della, true to her nature, opened her mouth, put one hand over it and with the other hand pointed toward the telephone.

Annie, whose back was to it, gave a shriek and swung round to meet whatever doom Della's open mouth and quaking finger indicated.

Seeing only the telephone she whispered, faint with relief, "I thought — I thought you saw — something."

"Him," Della said. "You forgot *him*."

"Oh, Lordy."

"You better phone him back."

"Oh, Lordy, he'll be mad."

But Annie did not give him a chance to be mad. She told him immediately and bluntly that his wife had disappeared.

"Have you gone crazy, Annie?" Andrew demanded.

"Plumb disappeared, Dr. Morrow, honestly."

"Annie, kindly . . ."

"Oh, I know how it sounds, Dr. Morrow, nobody can tell me how it sounds. Della and me, we're *scared.* We been through all the rooms except ours and there ain't a trace of her, I tell you."

"Where's my sister?" Andrew said. "Let me speak to her."

"She didn't come back yet."

"Then you two incompetents are there alone?"

"Della and me," Annie said huffily, "we may not have an education but we got eyes and Mrs. Morrow has plumb disappeared. Right after the man brought the box we heard her scream and I went up and she told me to beat it. And that's the last thing she said to me on this earth."

"I'll be right home," Andrew said. "Meanwhile don't get hysterical. Mrs. Morrow very likely went out for a walk."

"Without a *coat?*" Annie said, and paused slyly.

"What's this about a coat?"

"Her coats are all in her closet. Della and me, we looked and they're all there."

"See here, Annie," Andrew said in a calm voice, "don't get excited. You know Mrs. Morrow fairly well by this time. Has she ever done anything that wasn't practical and reasonable?"

"N-no, sir."

"Then hold the fort until I get there."

"Maybe it wasn't something she done,

maybe it was something somebody done *to* her."

But Andrew had already hung up. Slowly Annie did the same and turned to face a feverish-looking Della.

"But there's nobody here," Della said.

"Maybe not."

"Oh, you're trying to scare me again! What'd he say?"

"He's coming home."

"Right away?"

"That's what he said. He don't believe us. He says she went for a walk. A walk in this weather in a short-sleeved dress, I ask you. And anyway does she ever go for walks?"

"Not that I know of," Della agreed. "But you can't tell at her age."

"I'm sick of hearing about her age."

They were silent a moment. Then Della said wistfully, "We could talk about the emeralds again. You want to?"

"Sure."

"We'd keep one apiece. How many do you think there was in the first place?"

"Fifty," Annie said listlessly.

"Fifty, imagine that! They'd be worth a million. What'd be the very first thing you'd buy, Annie?"

"A dress, I guess."

"I'd buy a black-chiffon nightgown."

The game went on, but the emeralds had turned into green glass.

Shortly before six o'clock Andrew arrived home with Martin. Hand in hand, for moral support, the two girls came out into the hall.

"Well?" Andrew said, with a trace of irritation. "Mrs. Morrow back yet?"

Annie shook her head. "No, sir."

"You said over the phone that you looked through the whole house except your own rooms?"

"We didn't look there because what would she be doing up there? You think we should go up there now?"

"Don't bother," Andrew said and turned to Martin. "Run up to the third floor, will you, just as a precaution."

"All right." Martin flung his coat and hat on the hall table and ascended the steps, two at a time.

Andrew took off his own coat in a leisurely manner. "What are all the lights on for?"

"Della and me, we felt better with them on," Annie said. "Della's got bad nerves."

"It wasn't just me," Della muttered.

"Turn off some of the lights," Andrew said.

His refusal to get excited made the girls calmer. Della's mind began to function again and she went out to the kitchen to start preparing dinner, leaving Annie to tell about the man with the parcel.

Annie couldn't remember whether the man was short or tall, dark, or fair, young or old. She knew only that he was sinister.

"By sinister no doubt you mean shabby?" Andrew said dryly. "Go on."

"The light was dim and I didn't notice him much because he should've come to the back door."

Andrew listened patiently as she described the box and the conversation. But Annie noticed that he kept one eye on the steps waiting for Martin to return.

Martin came back, looking partly amused, partly exasperated.

"Crazy as it sounds," he said, "she's gone."

His father silenced him with a look and turned to Annie. "All right, Annie, you may go. It's simply a matter of waiting for Mrs. Morrow to come back."

"What gets me," Annie said, "is the coats."

"What coats?" Martin said.

"You may go, Annie," Andrew repeated sharply.

Annie left, and remarked to Della that never ever until today had Dr. Morrow or

Mrs. Morrow spoken roughly to her.

Left alone in the hall Andrew and Martin glanced uneasily at each other.

"Crazy as hell, isn't it?" Martin said. "A grown and capable woman goes out of the house and everyone begins to imagine things."

"If she went, she went without a coat. Annie says there is none missing. Come in here. I don't want those two to hear us."

They went into Andrew's den and closed the door.

"She might have slipped over to a neighbor's house," Martin said, avoiding his father's eye.

"She doesn't know the neighbors. Lucille's not like that."

"How do you know? She might do some calling that she doesn't tell you about."

Andrew blinked. "What are you implying?"

"Nothing. Just that you can't know everything about a person."

"That's true. But in fifteen years you get a fairly accurate impression, you can anticipate reactions." He reached for the decanter on his desk. "Drink?"

"Thanks," Martin said.

"This is practically the first time I've ever come home without having Lucille greet me. No doubt that sounds dull to you, Martin."

"Pretty dull," Martin said, and at the mere mention of dullness and constriction and boredom he felt incredibly vital and alive. He wanted to fling himself out of the chair, to stretch, to jump, to run, to make noises. He felt his muscles go taut, and he had to force himself to keep his feet still.

Andrew noticed the tension but misunderstood the cause.

"What did you mean, that Lucille might do some calling that she doesn't tell me about?"

"Good Lord, I wasn't slandering her. I simply meant that she wouldn't tell you every little thing she did for fear of boring you. She's a quiet person anyway."

"Yes. Annie said she screamed."

"Screamed?" Martin said. "Lucille? What about?"

"She wouldn't tell Annie." Andrew leaned his head on his hands. He looked grayer and more tired than Martin had ever seen him look before.

How old he is, Martin thought, how old and settled. Intolerant of age and inactivity, Martin began impatiently to move the stuff about on Andrew's desk. He emptied and then filled a pen, he rearranged some books, he scribbled his name on the blotter and he folded a page from the memo pad into a fan.

"Being a doctor's wife," Andrew said, "is a hard job. Being a second wife doesn't make it easier. Yet Lucille has never complained. What's that you're staring at?"

"Nothing," Martin said. "A piece of paper. Somebody's burned holes in it with a cigarette."

"Put it down then, and don't fidget. You're as jumpy as Edith."

"Odd."

"What?"

"These pictures. They look like my mother. Somebody's burned the eyes out."

"What? Give it to me." Andrew took the paper and looked at it briefly. "Nonsense. Not a bit like your mother."

"I think so."

"More implications, Martin?"

"Not at all," Martin said politely, and tossed the paper aside as if it suddenly bored him.

"You believe," Andrew said, "that Lucille drew pictures of Mildred and then mutilated them?"

"Oh, what does it matter?"

"It matters to me. If you like, when Lucille comes back home I'll ask her."

"Good Lord, no."

"I insist on asking her," Andrew said.

Martin pounded his fist on the desk. Nearly all of his arguments with his father left him with this feeling of helpless rage against Andrew's naivete. After twenty-five years of being a doctor Andrew seemed never to have lost his faith in human nature. Martin, who had no faith in anyone but himself and no religious convictions beyond the basic one that he was God, alternately respected and despised his father.

The two men watched each other across the width of the desk. The return of Lucille was now an issue between them, and their faces had a waiting look.

At six-thirty Edith arrived. She had left Polly and Giles dining at the Oak Room and had rushed home in the conviction that everything would go wrong in the house if she didn't.

The fact that everything had already gone wrong was explained to her vividly by Annie as soon as she opened the door. After the first shock was over Edith plunged into the mystery and upset the whole house with her splashing and churning.

It was Edith who discovered that Lucille's black-suede purse and the housekeeping money for the rest of the month were missing. Della and Annie vigorously denied going near the drawer where Lucille kept her purses. Edith believed them.

"So," she told Andrew, "Lucille must have taken it herself."

"But why?"

"I don't know. Perhaps she wanted to go out and buy something, that's the simplest explanation."

"She wasn't wearing a coat."

"Nonsense," Edith said. "I'm not pretending to know *why* she went out but I refuse to believe any sensible person would go out in this weather without a coat. She may have worn one of mine."

Edith's coats, however, were all found in her closet.

It was Della who backed up Edith's belief in what a sensible woman would do. Della had gone up to her room on the third floor to change her uniform. Her discarded one, tear-stained because Edith had called her a moron, she tossed into the closet. She saw that someone had disarranged the clothes.

A few minutes later she came down the stairs wailing.

"My money," she screamed at Edith. "My coat and money! She took it! She's a thief, a common thief!"

Twenty dollars and a reversible raincoat had been taken from Della's closet. The coat, beige gabardine on one side and red-plaid wool on the other, was practically new and not even a fifty-dollar check mended Della's broken heart.

Though the manner of Lucille's departure now seemed to be explained, for Edith the taking of Della's coat merely deepened the mystery.

"Why Della's coat?" she said. "Why not one of her own? It's as if — as if she was escaping and didn't want anyone to recognize her."

"No," Andrew said. "No, I don't believe it."

"And the money. . . . Yes, Andrew, she ran away."

"The girls swear they didn't hear her go out. They went upstairs and looked for her."

"That was when she got out," Edith said. "She ran up to hide in Della's room while they were looking through hers. When they went downstairs again and were searching the living room she came down with the coat and the purse and the money. . . ."

She put her hand over her eyes to blot out the picture. How vivid it seemed, how grotesquely easy it was for the mind to twist Lucille's placid smile into a crafty grin, to add slyness to the quiet eyes, and furtiveness to the sure slow movements of her body.

Perhaps I look like that to someone, Edith thought. We are all protected by a veil of trust. I must think of her as she was.

But the veil was already torn and the crafty grin and the furtiveness became clearer. Suspicions grew in Edith's mind like little extra eyes.

"And then," Edith said, "she simply went out the back door while the girls were in the living room."

"Simply," Andrew said with a sharp mirthless laugh. *"Simply!"*

Edith flushed. "I'm terribly sorry, Andrew."

"Sorry. Another magnificent understatement, my dear. I don't want you to be sorry for having spoken your mind. If you believe that my wife is a thief and perhaps worse, you can't help it. Any more than Martin can help it."

"I haven't said anything," Martin said. "Yet."

"Keep quiet, Martin," Edith said. She went over to Andrew and placed her hand on his shoulder. "Andrew, I'm sorry, I don't know what to think."

He smiled up at her, wryly. "Then why think? If Lucille went away she had a reason to go. She'll be back."

Edith and Martin exchanged glances over his head.

"And if she had a reason," Andrew continued, "she had a right to go. People should be allowed a certain freedom of movement. They shouldn't get the feeling that they are constantly required to be some place at some specific time. They should have certain periods when nothing whatever is expected from them."

"This is very like a lecture," Edith said coldly, "directed against me."

"Perhaps deservedly, Edith. You're a driver. You can't help it, I know, any more than I can help allowing myself to be driven, for the sake of peace."

"What has all this to do with Lucille?"

"Nothing," Andrew said. "Nothing at all. I was just talking."

"You aren't usually so talkative."

"I keep thinking," he said with gesture, "I keep thinking, suppose when she was up in her room she had a feeling that she was in a prison, that she must suddenly escape, that the very walls were a weight on her. When I feel like that I escape to my office, I run like a hare back to my pregnant women, my neurotic young girls, my ladies with cysts and sorrows and headaches and backaches and constipation. . . ."

"Really, Andrew!" Edith said, frowning.

"Women," Andrew said. "I don't know

how many there are in the world, but I think I've seen half of them and they're all constipated."

"Father had a couple of drinks before you came," Martin said.

"You *know* you can't drink, Andrew," Edith said, annoyed. "It goes to your head."

"Please go away, Edith. Please go away back and sit down some place."

But Edith refused. She was as incapable of sitting down as she was of keeping quiet. Pacing the room she went over all the facts again, returning in the end to the unanswerable question, *why?*

"Why?" Martin echoed. "Perhaps Father's right. She felt like that, and off she went."

Edith shook her head. "No, that's quite incredible. You know what a thoroughly sensible person Lucille is. If she felt like that she would simply have gone for a nice long walls or something."

"People aren't always capable of making sense," Andrew said in a strange voice. "There are forces — forces in the mind . . ." He leaned forward and fixed his eyes on her. "Look, Edith. See, it's like a jungle, the mind, dark and thick, with a million little paths that the light never reaches. You never know the paths are there until something pops out of one of them. Then, Edith, you might try to trace it back looking for its spoor and tracks, and you go so far, just so far, but the path is too twisted, too lightless, soundless, timeless . . ."

Edith was standing with her mouth open, and quite suddenly she began to cry. She cried not for Andrew's sake or Lucille's, but from sheer exasperation, because two people in whom she had placed her trust had betrayed her by stepping out of character. She saw Andrew as a dear little boy who suddenly and incongruously grows a long gray beard.

She brushed away her tears with the back of her hand, angrily conscious that Martin was looking at her with dismay, and Andrew with a kind of detached interest.

She averted her face and said stiffly, "You're implying that Lucille has gone crazy?"

"No," Andrew said, his voice mild again, and a little tired. "No. I think she . . ."

"It would be far more to the point to investigate the man who brought the parcel to her. However dark a jungle my mind is, Andrew, I am still capable of logic. Whatever prompted Lucille to go away, the man with the parcel is connected with it. That's the only out-of-the-ordinary thing that's happened to her."

"No," Andrew said, "there's one other, isn't there? Giles Frome."

"What on earth would Giles have to do with it?"

"Probably nothing. Like yourself I'm simply being logical."

"Good Lord," Martin said. "I haven't been able to get a word in. I agree with Edith about the man with the parcel. The trouble is finding him."

"What are the police for?" Edith said.

"The police," Martin said dryly, "are for finding people."

CHAPTER 4

"My wife," Andrew said, "has disappeared."

"Ah," Inspector Bascombe said, and folded his big square hands on the desk in front of him. He was a heavy, sour-looking man with bitter little eyes that seemed to fling acid on everyone they saw.

He was thinking, so your wife has disappeared. Yours and a couple of thousand others'. Including mine. With an electrician from Hull.

"The details, please," he said without inflection.

"They're rather peculiar."

Why, sure they are. Bascombe thought. The details are always peculiar. What isn't peculiar is how the wives turn up again when they're left flat and broke. Except mine.

He said, "Sit down, Dr. Morrow, and make yourself comfortable. There's rather a long form to be filled out, her description and so forth."

Bascombe watched him as he sat down. He felt very glad that Morrow's wife had disappeared because Morrow was the kind of man he hated most, next to electricians. Goddam whiskey ad, he thought. Men of achievement, men of tomorrow. Even the top drawer have women troubles, what a goddam shame.

Thinking of whiskey ads reminded him of the bottle of Scotch he had hidden in the files. He tried to forget it again by being extra crisp and businesslike.

"Name?"

"Lucille Alexandra Morrow."

He wrote rapidly. Lucille Alexandra Morrow. Female. White. Age forty-five. Red-gold hair, long; blue eyes, fair skin, no distinguishing marks.

The red-gold hair reminded him of the Scotch again. His hand jerked across the paper leaving a spray of ink.

He looked up to see if Morrow had noticed, but Morrow wasn't watching him. He had his eyes fixed on the lettering on the glass door — Department of Missing Persons.

"Kind of fascinates you, doesn't it," Bascombe laughed. "I read it a million times a day."

Make it two million, and every time, I get a cold wet feeling in the gut. The Missing Persons. Some of them will never be found, some will come back by themselves, drunk or sick or broke or just tired. And some of them will come up from the mud at the bottom of the river in April or May, the ladies on their backs, and the gentlemen face down.

He got up abruptly, and the pen rolled across the desk. Muttering something under his breath he went into the next room and closed the door behind him.

Sergeant D'arcy, a small rosy-cheeked young man who looked a little too elegant in his uniform, glanced up from his desk.

"Yes, sir?" he said.

"Get the hell in there," Bascombe said thickly. "Some guy's lost his wife. Take it all down. I feel rotten."

"Yes, sir," D'arcy said, riffling some papers efficiently. "Is there anything I can do, sir?"

"What I've already told you to do."

"I meant aside from . . ."

"Scram, lovely."

When D'arcy had gone Bascombe removed the bottle of Scotch from the back of the Closed Cases M to N file. D'arcy, who was listening, heard the gurgle of liquid, and thought, poor Bascombe, he had a truly great brain but he was drinking on duty again and would have to be reported.

To Andrew, D'arcy presented his fine

teeth, brushed for five minutes in the morning and five at night.

"Inspector Bascombe had a slight touch of indigestion. He asked me to continue for him."

He picked up the form, noticing at once the spray of ink. *Poor Bascombe.*

"Now, of course," he said, "We require a few more details. Has Mrs. Morrow ever gone away like this before?"

"Never."

"There is no evidence of coercion?"

"None," Andrew hesitated, "that I know of."

"Did she have any reason for leaving, to your knowledge, any domestic upsets and the like?"

"None."

"No other man involved, of course?"

Andrew looked at him with cold dislike. "There has never been any other man involved in her life except her first husband, George Lanvers. He's been dead for nearly twenty years."

"We have to ask certain questions," D'arcy said, flushing. "We really do."

"I understand that."

"We . . ." D'arcy paused and looked hopefully toward the door.

He wished Bascombe would come back.

He didn't like asking people questions, he didn't even like the Department. Or Bascombe.

He cocked his head, listening for sounds in the outer office. As soon as he heard one he excused himself and went out.

Bascombe had gone, but three people were waiting on the benches along the wall. One of them, an elderly well-dressed woman, D'arcy was able to dismiss immediately. She had come every day for nearly six months looking for her son.

"Sorry, Mrs. Granger," D'arcy said.

She seemed quite cheerful. "No news from Barney yet? He'll turn up. One of these days he'll be turning up and surprising me."

She went out briskly. The two men rose and came over to D'arcy. They were in the fur business and they had sold a mink coat to a man named Wilson for cash. The cash had turned out to be counterfeit and Wilson and the coat were missing.

D'arcy referred them, with a superior smile, to another department. But he wasn't feeling superior. He had the sinking sensation that he always got when he was required to do any thinking for himself.

The door opened and Bascombe came back in.

"The doctor still here?" he asked.

"Yes, sir. It seems to be a very interesting case."

"Aren't they all."

"I wish — I think you should talk to him personally."

Bascombe's face was flushed and his eyes were a little glassy.

"Thanks for the advice, D'arcy."

"Well, but I really mean it, sir. Dr. Morrow looks as if he might have considerable influence."

"The only kind of influence I care about comes in quart bottles," Bascombe said, but he laughed, almost good-naturedly, and went back into his own office.

It was nearly noon when he came out again with Dr. Morrow. Morrow left immediately, looking, D'arcy noticed, pretty grim.

Bascombe was smiling all over his face. "A very nice case. The lady disappeared with all the money she could get her hands on, wearing one of her maid's coats. A reversible coat. Get it?"

"No, sir."

"Plaid on one side, beige on another. She can switch them around and make it harder for us to find her. Inference, she's not coming back and she doesn't want to be found. So just for the hell of it we'll find her.

Get your notebook."

"Yes, sir."

"All right. The usual checkups first, hospital and morgue and her bank — Bloor and Ossington Branch of the Bank of Toronto. I think you'll draw blanks there. Morrow's going to send over a couple of studio portraits by messenger. Meanwhile, start calling beauty parlors."

"All of the beauty parlors?" D'arcy said faintly.

"Use your noodle and you won't have to. If the woman is really in earnest about disappearing, she'll probably try to disguise her most distinctive feature, her hair, and then grab a train or bus for out-of-town."

"And the bus terminals and stations being mostly in the south and west I'm to try those sections first?"

"Amazing," Bascombe said. "Beauty *and* brains you have, D'arcy. I'm going out to lunch. Be back later."

When he had gone D'arcy did a little checking-up on his own and discovered that the bottle of Scotch was missing from the file.

"Poor Bascombe," he said sadly. "I'll have to report him. It's my duty."

He didn't want to report Bascombe, who was a fine figure of a man, really.

He sat down at his desk and picked up the telephone directory. D'arcy was at his best on a telephone, he could forget how small he was and how the other policemen didn't like him and kept shunting him back and forth from one department to another.

While he was working Kirby came in. He was a big loose-jointed young man who spent half his time around the morgue and the hospitals.

"It's about time someone appeared," D'arcy said. "I haven't had my lunch. I'm hungry."

"Too bad." Kirby took off his hat and stretched and yawned. "Where's Bascombe?"

"I'm sure I don't know. He doesn't confide in me."

"He owes me five bucks on the Macgregor girl. I found her this morning. She's in a ward at Western with a nice case. Says she got it in a washroom."

"People," D'arcy said primly, "should behave themselves."

Pointedly, he returned to the telephone. He worked nearly all afternoon with one eye on the door, waiting for Bascombe to come back.

At four-thirty he became quite excited by a telephone conversation he had with Miss

Flack, who owned and operated the Sally Ann hairdressing parlor in Sunnyside. He tried to get Bascombe's apartment on the wire. Nobody answered.

"I'll report him," D'arcy whispered "I really will. It's *high time.*"

He went up to Sands' office.

The Allen Hotel is on a little street off College. A red-brick building, caked with soot, it has passed through many phases in its long life. It has been, in turn, a private hospital, a barracks, an apartment house, and a four-bit flophouse. The Liquor Act was passed just in time to save it from the wreckers. A few licks of paint, extra chairs and tables, a new neon sign and a license to sell beer and wine transformed the old building into the Allen Hotel, a fairly prosperous tavern with a dubious clientele. The clientele was kept under control by a large tough bartender and a number of printed prohibitions which were strictly enforced: No checks cashed. No credit. No spitting.

There were other prohibitions also, but these were not printed on signs. The bartender attended to them himself. He would sidle up behind a customer and say gently, "No pimps," or sometimes, "No fairies."

Not that he gave a damn about them but

he was afraid of the health and liquor inspectors that came around. He didn't want the place to close up. With his salary and the takeoff he got from the beer salesmen he was buying a house out in the east end for his family.

Through his efforts the Allen Hotel got quite a good name with the various inspectors. They didn't bother much about it any more. The word was passed around, and a number of people who didn't want to come in contact with the law began to use the rooms upstairs. It was ironical, but in one way it wasn't so bad. The bartender soaked up information like a blotter. Some of it he sold, some of it he gave away to his friend Sands. From Sands, in return, he got the pleasant feeling that he was on the good side of the law, and that if a time came when he wasn't, there was at least one honest policeman in the world.

He took personal pride in Sands and followed all his cases in the newspapers. Whenever Sands came in for a drink or some information the bartender's face would take on a sly, conspiratorial smile because here were all these bums drinking side by side with a real detective and not knowing it. Sometimes he was so pleased he had to go into the can and roar with laughter.

Today he wasn't so pleased. He leaned across the counter and spoke out of the side of his mouth.

"Mr. Sands."

"Hello, Bill," Sands said, sitting on the bar stool.

"Mr. Sands, there's a friend of yours in the back booth. Been here nearly all day. I would sure like to lose him."

"Bascombe?"

The bartender nodded. "This is no kind of place for a policeman to get drunk in. I wouldn't want anything to happen to Mr. Bascombe." He grinned suddenly. "Not unless it was fatal."

"I'll talk to him," Sands said. "Bring me a small ale."

He got off the bar stool, a thin tired-looking middle-aged man with features that fitted each other so perfectly that few people could remember what he looked like. His clothes blended in with the rest of him, they were gray and rather battered and limp. He moved unobtrusively to the back of the room.

Bascombe was sitting alone in the booth with his head in his hands.

"Bascombe."

No answer.

"Bascombe." Sands knocked away

Bascombe's elbows. Bascombe's head lolled and then righted itself. His eyes didn't open.

"Don't mind if I do," Bascombe said huskily. "Make it double."

Sands sat down on the other side of the booth and sipped his ale patiently. Pretty soon Bascombe blinked his eyes open and looked across the table at him.

"Oh, for Christ's sake," he said, "it's you. Go away, Sands, go away, my boy. You have this elfin habit of appearing suddenly. I don't like it. It's upsetting."

"D'arcy's been looking for you," Sands said.

"Trouble with D'arcy is his brassiere's too tight."

"You'd better come to and listen. D'arcy's got his knife in you."

"Sure, I know," Bascombe said. "I got sick of him following me around and maybe I talked a little rough to him."

"He reported you for drinking on duty."

Bascombe blinked again. "Who to?"

"To me."

"As long as it was to you."

"Maybe next time it won't be," Sands said. "How many times is this that Ellen's left you?"

"Five," Bascombe said, his face twisting.

"Yeah. Five. In three years."

"I suppose it's no use my pointing out that Ellen is a little tramp?" Sands said dryly. "She isn't housebroken. You can't do anything with that kind but leave them. Get a divorce. Bascombe." Bascombe didn't answer. "If it'll make it easier for you, I could have you transferred to another department. That's D'arcy's suggestion."

"That goddam little . . ."

"Sure, but even D'arcy hits it on the button sometimes. I think he's right. He said you were fussed up this A.M. over some doctor whose wife is missing."

"I can't help thinking of Ellen."

"That's what I mean. Incidentally D'arcy thinks he's traced the doctor's wife as far as some hairdressing shop down near Sunnyside."

"How do you know so much about it?"

"Oh, I've been interested in the Morrow family for a long time," Sands said, and picked up his glass again. "For about sixteen years, I guess. Get your coat on."

"What for? I'm not going any place."

"Yes, you are. I spent an hour and a half looking for you. I told D'arcy that you were out doing some work for me and that I'd pick you up and take you down to Sunnyside. Get your coat."

"You're an easy guy to hate, Sands. You're so goddam right all the time, aren't you, so goddam sure of yourself."

Sands said nothing. He never talked about himself, and he didn't like to listen to other people talk about him. It seemed unreal to him, as if they must be talking about someone else.

He left Bascombe struggling with his overcoat and went ahead to the bar.

The bartender was rinsing glasses. He stopped work and wiped his hands.

"He going with you, Mr. Sands?"

"Yes."

"Jesus," Bill said. "You must be a regular one of those guys that the rats followed."

"A nice description," Sands said. Great rats, small rats, lean rats, brawny rats . . .

"Human nature is sure a funny thing," Bill said. "Take me, how big I am, and take you, how small you are, and here I couldn't do a thing with Mr. Bascombe, and he follows you like a lamb. You must have plenty muscle that don't show."

"Any eight-year-old could knock me off my pins."

"Jesus, Mr. Sands, you shouldn't talk like that." Bill was offended. "It might get around."

Bascombe came up. He had his overcoat

buttoned wrong but he walked straight and his voice had lost its thickness.

"Bye, Billy-boy," he said to the bartender. "When they kick me off the force let's make a date in a dark alley."

"I'd like that fine," the bartender said thoughtfully.

When the two policemen had gone Bill returned to the glasses. Officially the Allen Hotel had been open all day but it was after dark that business got heavy. Bill had a couple of waiters who came in around seven. When there was a rush on he helped serve but most of the night he spent sizing up the customers and easing out drunks and keeping an eye on the money. At the Allen any bill over five dollars was automatically considered phony until Bill had passed on it.

Tuesday night was the slowest of the week and only one thing happened that Bill felt Sands should know about. A little ex-con and hophead called Greeley came in with a red-headed fat woman. The woman Bill recognized as a floozie from a house down the street. But it took him several minutes to recognize Greeley. He had on a brand-new topcoat and a new green fedora. But the newest thing about Greeley was his expression. He acted like a millionaire who had to rub shoulders with a rough mob.

"Well, well," Bill said. "*Mister* Greeley. Pardon me while I catch my breath. And is this charming lady Mrs. Greeley?"

The woman giggled, but Greeley gave him a sour look and led the woman to one of the tables. Bill followed them.

"If I'd known you was coming, Mr. Greeley, I'd have got out my Irish-lace tablecloth, sure as hell."

"Champagne," Greeley said, and sat down without taking off his hat and coat.

"Teaspoon or tablespoon?" Bill said. The woman giggled again.

Greeley laid a fifty-dollar bill on the table.

Bill did everything to the bill but chew it up, and it still looked good.

When the bottle of champagne was gone Greeley had lost his sour look and was beginning to talk big. Bill stood as near the table as he could and now and then he caught a snatch of Greeley's talk.

"I don't want to spend the rest of my life bouncing in and out of Kingston for rolling drunks and picking pockets. Listen, Sue, I'm on to something. You climb on the wagon with me, baby."

"Sure," the woman said. "Sure. Anything you say."

"The kinda life we lead we don't get respect for ourselves. Something high class, that's what I got, something classy and steady. Look around this dump, look at it."

The woman obliged.

"Ain't it a dump?" Greeley said. "Couple of days ago this was my idea of a big night, getting tanked in a dump like this with a chance to get fixed up after."

"Well, what are we sitting here for if you're so high class?"

"Saying good-bye," Greeley said solemnly. "Saying good-bye to a crappy life like this. From now on you'll be covered with diamonds."

"The hell with diamonds. I want a square meal."

Greeley ordered a couple of hamburgers and another bottle of champagne.

The woman ate the hamburgers, biting on them as if her teeth hurt.

Three soldiers at the bar began to sing and Bill couldn't hear what Greeley was saying now. But he guessed it was the same kind of stuff. Greeley was leaning across the table being very intense while the woman chewed and watched him with a where-have-I-heard-this-before expression in her eyes.

Around ten they got up to go out and Bill noticed that Greeley's pants were badly frayed at the bottom. He hurried over to the till to test the fifty-dollar bill again.

Greeley saw him and flung him a contemptuous smile. Bill followed him to the door.

"Good night, *Mister* Greeley," he said. "You'll be back, we hope not."

The woman giggled and said, "Honest, you're a scream."

Greeley grabbed her arm. "You never laugh at nothing *I* say."

The woman pushed him away coolly. "At you I'm laughing all the time. I just gotta stop myself or I'd die."

"Good-bye, Wisenheim," Greeley said to Bill, opening the door. "Come and see me at the Royal York."

"They still taking on dishwashers? I bet you look cute in an apron."

A final giggle from the woman and then the door slammed.

Wish my wife would laugh like that at everything I say, Bill thought. She's got no sense of humor.

He went over to the soldiers. "Better quiet down, boys. I just saw a couple of M.P.s go past the door."

The soldiers quieted, and Tuesday night went on.

CHAPTER 5

On Tuesday Edith quarreled with nearly everyone in the house. She began with Andrew, who told her at breakfast time that he was going to report Lucille's disappearance to the police.

Edith raged and wept. It was too humiliating, it was too shameful, how would they ever hold their heads up again.

Andrew had left without even bothering to argue. Frustrated, Edith turned her anger on Martin. How *could* Martin go to the office when they needed him, he must stay home, it was his duty . . .

Directly after breakfast Martin too left the house.

The most violent quarrel was in the evening. Edith was in the living room with Polly and Giles. She suggested that the wedding be postponed.

Polly gave her a long hard stare. "What for?"

"It wouldn't look right if you were married at a time like this."

"It wouldn't look right to whom?" Polly said. "You? Lucille?"

"People will talk."

"People always do. This is Giles' last furlough before he goes overseas."

"I know," Edith said tragically. "I know it's a terrible thing to have it spoiled like this. But couldn't you wait just a few days? Perhaps Lucille will be back then."

"I don't care a damn about Lucille," Polly said. "I never have. The only way I've been able to live in the same house with her was to ignore her, not to let her spoil things for me. Well, she's not going to spoil them now."

Giles tried not to listen to the two women. He looked down at his hands, hardly recognizing them as his own he felt so unreal and formless. He seemed to be moving through a nightmare, without the power to wake up and without the strength to protect himself against the dim shapes of danger. Sometimes the house was like a box and he was alone in it and on the ceiling of the box there were shadows without cause and the walls moved slightly, in and out, as if the box were breathing. Sometimes he stopped to listen to it, and he heard his own breathing, surely it must be his own, but it sounded as if someone were breathing along with him in rhythm that wasn't quite perfect.

When he went into a room it always

seemed that someone had just left it. The air was stirring, and the door quivered.

"She's been very good to you," Edith was saying shrilly. "You shouldn't talk like that about her in front of Giles."

"I talk the way I want to. I don't fake things."

"Nobody listens to me in this house! I won't have it! I forbid you to be married until we find out about Lucille."

"I don't need permission," Polly said. She turned her back, but Edith's voice clawed at her ears.

"What do you know about Giles? What do you know about him?"

"I guess there isn't much to know," Giles said, and attempted to smile. "I mean, I realize how queer it looks that Mrs. Morrow should disappear the day after I arrive. But I assure you . . ."

"You must be crazy, Edith," Polly said in a cold flat voice. "It's bad enough that Giles should have to be here at such a time, without being accused by you."

"She said he reminded her of someone," Edith cried, flinging herself violently into this new idea. "You can't tell about people, you can't believe anyone, you can't trust . . ."

Her voice snapped. She turned abruptly and ran out of the room, the sleeves of her dress fluttering. She looked like a great flapping bird with broken wings.

"Giles."

"Yes?"

"Let's get out of here. Now. Tonight."

"Can we?"

"No one can stop us. We'll just leave. Giles, go up and pack. We can go to a hotel."

"All right." The ceiling of the box seemed to open and clear cool air rushed in. "All right, we'll just leave."

"Oh, Giles."

The telephone in the hall began to ring.

"It surely looks like her," said Miss Betty Flack. "It surely does. But I can't be sure. I mean if it's important, with the police in it and all, then I can't be sure." Miss Flack handed back the photographs and added thoughtfully, "But it surely looks like her."

Over Miss Flack's platinum curls Bascombe and Sands exchanged glances.

"What I mean is," said Miss Flack with an elegant gesture, "I *think* it's her, all right. She came in just when I was closing the shop up and wanted to know if I did hair-cutting. Well, naturally I do, though my real specialty is cold waves."

"You cut her hair?" Sands said, gently

guiding Miss Flack's mind back from the cold waves.

"I gave her a feather cut. Did you see *For Whom the Bell Tolls*? Well, like that. The girl in it, I mean. Mrs. Smith, she said that was her name, she didn't seem to care how I cut it, just sat there holding her purse. I noticed her shoes were wet and I like to make a little joke now and then with my customers, so I asked her, laughing-like, if she'd been in swimming down at the lake. She didn't think it was funny," Miss Flack said, adding fairly, "Maybe it wasn't."

"Didn't she say anything at all?" Sands asked.

"Just about how cold it was. I surely felt sorry for her with such a flimsy little coat on. She was such a *lady,* if you know what I mean, and so sort of *desperate* looking. I thought to myself at the time, maybe her husband drinks or something." Miss Flack had another of her thoughtful pauses. "He certainly *looked* as if he drank."

"Oh," Sands said, and Bascombe's hands twitched as if they wanted to get around Miss Flack's throat and choke something out of her. "Her husband came with her?"

"Not exactly. I mean, I don't know if he *came* with her, but when she went out I stood at the door getting a breath of fresh air and I saw this man waiting across the street. Mrs. Smith stopped and talked to him for a minute and then she walked ahead and he followed her. I remember thinking to myself at the time, isn't it a caution what women marry sometimes. She was so tall and handsome and he was just a little fellow."

"A little fellow," Sands said, and thought back sixteen years to the last time he'd seen Andrew Morrow. Morrow was about six foot three. Even making allowances for the fact that the light had been dim and Miss Flack's memory was of the vague and romantic order, Sands was sure that the man Mrs. Morrow met across the street had not been her husband.

It was easy enough to check. Sands asked Miss Flack for a telephone and while he was sitting in the booth looking in the directory for Morrow's number, he heard Miss Flack tell Bascombe that she herself was single, had a half-interest in the beauty parlor and liked great big men.

Sands dialed.

The door into the hall was still open and Polly and Giles heard Della answer the phone and then trot down the hall. A minute later Andrew came to the phone. They heard him say, "Hello. Yes, this is Dr. Morrow."

"Well," Polly said sharply, "do we listen or do we talk? Or do you go up and pack?"

"I will if you want me to."

"If!" Polly said bitterly. "Oh, well, nothing like a telephone ringing for breaking up moods, is there, Giles?" She clenched her hands and began to swear in an undertone. "Damn, damn, damn, damn."

Andrew's voice crept into the room. "Sands? No, I'm sorry I don't think I do remember. Sands." A pause, a change of tone. "Oh. Oh, yes." He cleared his throat. "I'm — I'm very glad you were able to — to get that far. S-sunnyside? No, I was at home. The maids were frightened and called me home from the office. Will you hold the line, please?"

Gray-lipped, he came to the door of the living room and shut it without saying anything.

"It's the police," Giles said. "I suppose they've found out something. I — Polly, what's the matter?"

Her shoulders were shaking and a film had spread over her eyes like ice over a river.

"Giles, it's that man, it's that same one. Sands. He came with a lot of men and I could see them from my window going over the snow. Parts of it were like red slush."

"I don't understand . . ."

"One of them, Sands, came in the house and sat over there, in that chair. He just sat and looked at us, at Martin and me, for a long time. Martin kept laughing. I don't know why, but he kept on laughing and laughing."

She rose unsteadily and walked across the room and stood in front of Mildred's portrait. For a minute the implacable brown eyes stared into the mild and vacuous blue eyes.

Giles looked after her, puzzled. "Who is that?"

"My mother."

"Oh."

"She was quite young when she died." Polly turned around. Her face was hard and merciless. "Probably it's just as well. She was the type who would have run to fat."

Giles didn't want to look at her. He was always a little frightened of her. In their relationship it was Polly who was the realist, he the dreamer; she was the leader, he the follower.

"I'd better go up and tell Martin," she said. "He'll want to know."

"Do you still want to leave? Do you want me to go up and pack?"

"What?" she said, as if she had forgotten

about it, had even forgotten him and who he was and why he was there. "I'll have to tell Martin."

"It was in the winter," Sands said. "For a couple of months there'd been stories of children being chased in the park on their way home from school. The stories were vague and nobody was ever arrested. Then one night Mildred Morrow was out visiting a friend. She didn't come home."

Sands paused. "The friend was a widow who lived in the next house. Her name was Lucille Lanvers. Her statement was that Mildred had left her house before eleven o'clock, ostensibly to go home. Dr. Morrow was at the hospital on a confinement case and when he returned at one o'clock Mildred Morrow still hadn't come home. He called his sister Edith who was in bed and they went over to Mrs. Lanvers' house. The three of them looked around the park for an hour or so and then called in the police.

"About six o'clock the next morning we found Mildred Morrow lying against a tree with her head split open. Her purse and some valuable jewels were missing. The weapon wasn't found but we were pretty sure it was an axe. There was a heavy snowfall during the night, the body was almost completely covered and while there were indentations in the snow where foot tracks had been they were useless to us."

"Who had the case?" Bascombe said.

"Inspector Hannegan. I was a patrolman at the time. I rode a motorcycle."

"Oh, for Christ's sake," Bascombe said. "A motorcycle."

Sands smiled quietly. "Sure. Hannegan figured the case was simple robbery and he had a great time hauling in all the boys who'd ever stolen a balloon from the dime store. As a favor, he let me fool around with the case from another angle. I got nowhere. There seemed to be no motive for the crime except robbery. I talked to the family and to Mrs. Lanvers, but I had no official standing. Then Hannegan got tired of the case and closed it after a few weeks."

"What was your verdict?"

"I had none. Dr. Morrow had an alibi. His sister Edith puzzled me, she's one of these rather unstable people, and I had an idea that she was jealously fond of her brother and probably preferred him without a wife. Mrs. Lanvers was a quiet restrained woman, quite plain-looking, not as pretty as she is now, if her photographs don't lie. She was Mildred Morrow's best friend, and here again there was no motive but the vaguely possible one that she wanted Mildred's husband."

"And got him."

"Yes, but it's not unusual for a man to marry his wife's best friend. It's happening all the time, especially in cases like this where the man was profoundly in love with his wife. Morrow was crazy about Mildred. He was very sick for a long time after she was killed."

"And Lucille nursed him, I suppose," Bascombe said with a cynical smile.

"I don't know," Sands said. "But it was the children who worried me most. I don't know much about children and I found their reactions very queer. The girl was ten or eleven at the time. She acted as though nothing had happened and whenever I asked her a question she would stare at me and pretend she hadn't heard. The boy was a couple of years older, going to Upper Canada College at the time, he acted wild and crazy. He laughed a great deal and offered to fight me. He said he'd take me on with one hand tied behind his back provided I promised to keep clear of his spine which he'd had broken once in a football game."

"What happened to him?"

"He's now literary editor of the *Review.*"

"My God!"

"The only one of the family I've seen since is the girl, Polly. I came across her three years ago in court. She was testifying in some charity case. She recognized me and turned her head away."

"Funny she remembered you."

"Yes. Funny. Her father didn't when I phoned. Anyway, Hannegan closed the investigation and I was called off. Now I think it's opening again." He looked across at Bascombe. "Don't you?"

"Yeah," Bascombe said.

Miss Flack emerged from the small cubicle where she'd been gilding the lily.

"It surely is nice of you to offer to drive me home," she said. "To tell the honest truth I was scared to death when you said you were policemen. Now I'm not a *bit* scared."

"Good for you," Sands said.

Miss Flack was deposited at her apartment.

"What now?" Bascombe said.

"We look around."

"I think somebody told me once that Toronto was fifteen miles east and west and nine miles north and south."

"Is that a fact," Sands said.

"What I want to know is who's holding the baby, you or me?"

"We're sharing it until it's old enough to choose." The car shot ahead almost as if it knew what direction to take, like a well-trained horse. "I want to get to Mrs. Morrow first."

Mr. Greeley and his lady friend were at a dime-a-dance hall out on the pier. Neither of them felt at home. The place was too classy. Greeley was ashamed to take off his overcoat and show his old suit. By the end of the second dance the sweat was pouring down his neck and the effects of the champagne were wearing off. Greeley needed something stronger than champagne.

"Let's get the hell out of here," he said.

"What for?" the woman said. "I'm having a swell time."

"Hell, if it's rear-bumping you want you can get it in a street car and cheaper."

"We just get some place and then you want to go."

"I got a date, anyway. Come on."

He walked out, not even looking around to see if she followed.

When they were outside she said, "You got no manners, Eddy."

She buttoned her coat. The lake slapped at the pier with cold contemptuous hate.

"Jesus, Eddy, let's go home."

"Quit crabbing."

"I don't like it here."

"Well, for Christ's sake, wait a minute."

He pushed aside the flap of his overcoat, and stabbed something into his thigh through his clothes. His thigh felt sore but his mind began to see things right again, he had the right perspective now. Life was a stinker, but he, Greeley, had it licked.

Me, Greeley.

It was two o'clock in the morning when Sands called up again. Andrew hadn't gone to bed, he was sitting in his den with a book in his lap.

"Yes?" he said into the phone.

"Dr. Morrow? Inspector Sands. Could you get dressed . . ."

"I am dressed. What's happened?"

"I'm at the Lakeview Hotel. It's on Bleacher Street, right off the Boulevard, west of Sunnyside. Your — your wife is here."

"Yes . . . yes . . ." It was as if something had split inside his head and he had to talk above a terrible roaring. "Is she — she's all right?"

"She's alive," Sands said.

"She's sick, then? You say she's *sick?* I . . ."

Edith appeared at the door of the den, wrapped in an old plaid bathrobe. "What is it, Andrew? Tell me this instant! What is the matter?"

"I'm coming right away," Andrew said and laid down the phone.

"I'm going with you," Edith said. "Whatever it is I'm going with you, you can't face it alone."

Andrew looked at her, but he couldn't see her properly. She was just a blur of colors, a whirling chart of colors without form or meaning or substance. He didn't even feel his own hand pushing her aside, and though his legs moved, his feet didn't seem to touch the floor.

His eyes functioned but only if he looked at one thing at a time, one separate stationary thing, the door, the instrument bag packed and ready in the front seat of the car, a street lamp, a house, a tree.

She sat upright in a chair. Beside her the steam radiator was turned on and gave off blasts of noise and heat that smelled of paint. But her face remained cold and waxy and her eyes frozen.

"Mrs. Morrow . . ."

(There is a man in my room. Is it my room? No. Yes, my room. One man and another man. Two men.)

". . . I've phoned your husband. He's coming right away."

(What a lot of men in my room and so much talk.)

"If there's anything I could get you . . ."

(They might be talking to me.)

Bascombe shifted uneasily. "I don't think she hears you."

(But I do. You're making a mistake, young man. Young man? Old man? Two, anyway. Two, two.)

"Mrs. Morrow, I'd like to help you. If you can remember what happened to you . . ."

An expression moved across her face, softly, like a cat walking. She knew she must be clever now, these were her enemies.

(She was in the lake, she was swimming, and the water was cold and dark and the waves passionate against her and so strong. She saw a hand stretched out to help her, she reached for the hand and it pushed her savagely away, down, down, down, so black, so dying, dying.)

"Mrs. Morrow, here is your husband."

"Lucille — Lucille, darling . . ."

He came into the sweltering room. She turned her head very slowly and saw him hold out his hand to her.

She began to scream. The screams came

out of her throat smoothly, almost effortlessly, like a song from a bird.

When the ambulance came she was still screaming.

The ambulance neglected to pick up Mr. Greeley. The headlights just missed him.

He was sitting in the alley behind the hotel propped up against the wall. The wind from the lake stabbed at his face but Greeley didn't mind it. Life was a stinker but he, Greeley, had it licked. The night was dark but full of bright dreams — warm women, silk, thick soft fur, velvet hills and soft snug places.

Dreaming, he passed into sleep and sleeping into death.

PART TWO

The Fox

CHAPTER 6

She felt safe again. Behind her there was an iron gate and a hundred doors that locked with a big key. One of the nurses kept the key in the palm of her hand all the time.

There were no steps, only inclines that you walked up with someone beside you talking pleasantly and impersonally, and then finally the last door, the last clink of a key and the enemy was shut out. The room had windows but no one could get in through them. On both sides there was steel mesh.

She went immediately to the windows and felt the mesh, knowing that the nurse was watching her and would report it to the superintendent. But she had to know the room was safe and the feel of the mesh under her fingers was reassuring.

"It's strong, isn't it?" she said.

"Oh, yes," the nurse said cheerfully. She was young, with blonde curls and a pretty smile. She looked trim and efficient, but her eyes seemed to be laughing as though they lived a secret giddy life of their own. "I'm Miss Scott."

"Miss Scott," Lucille repeated.

"We'll just unpack your clothes now and put them away, Mrs. — Morrow."

"Mrs. Morrow."

"You'll be sharing this room with Miss Cora Green. Miss Green is down in the library at the moment. I'm sure you'll like her very much. We all do."

She began to unpack Lucille's clothes, keeping the key flat in the palm of her left hand. She did not turn her back to Lucille or take her eyes off her, but her vigilance was unobtrusive. She talked pleasantly and steadily. When Lucille finally noticed how closely she was being watched she did not resent it. Miss Scott was so smooth. She gave the impression that she was being merely careful, not suspicious, cautious but not in the least mistrustful.

"What a pretty blue dress," Miss Scott said. "Almost matches your eyes, doesn't it? I think we'll save that one for the movie night."

"I didn't know I was to share a room."

"We find it's better to have two people in a room. It's not so lonely. And you'll love Miss Green. She makes us all laugh."

"I wanted to be by myself."

"Of course you may feel like that at first. Would you mind handing me another hanger, Mrs. Morrow?"

Lucille moved automatically. The familiar act of hanging up one of her own dresses made her feel more at home. She picked up another hanger.

Miss Scott observed her. "Perhaps you'd like to finish up by yourself, Mrs. Morrow? Then you'll know where everything is."

"All right."

"We let everyone help herself as much as possible. We like to feel that each suite is a little community . . ."

"I don't want to see the others." The others, the crazy ones. "I want to be by myself."

"You'll feel a little strange at first, but we find our system is the best."

It was Lucille's first contact with the dominant "we." We, the nurses: we, the doctors, the brass keys, the steel mesh: we, the iron gate, the fence: we, the people, society: we the world.

"There are four rooms to each suite," Miss Scott said. "Two to a room. We try to put people of similar background together."

From somewhere outside the door a woman began to moan, "Give me more food and more clotherings." The voice was weak but distinct.

"That's Mrs. Hammond," Miss Scott

said briskly. "Don't pay any attention to her, she has plenty to eat and to wear."

"Give me more food and more clotherings."

"That's all she ever says," Miss Scott added.

"Give me . . ."

Lucille bent over the suitcase, as if her body had flowed suddenly out of her dress and the dress itself was ready to fold itself up in the suitcase and go home.

"Do you feel ill, Mrs. Morrow?"

There was a blur in front of her eyes and beyond the blur words dangled and danced, and beyond the thickness that clothed her ears voices spoke, out of turn, out of time.

Give me more food. People of similar background. Mrs. Morrow, here is your husband. More clotherings. What a pretty blue dress. Do you feel ill, Mrs. Morrow? Do you feel ill? Ill? Ill?

"No," she said.

"Just a little upset, eh?" Miss Scott said. "We expect that. Perhaps you'd like me to leave you alone for a minute or two until you get used to the room. I'll go down to the library and get Miss Green. Here, you'll find this blue chair very comfortable."

"Are you going to lock my door? I want my door locked."

"We never lock individual doors during the day."

"I want my door . . ."

"Tonight, when you're all tucked in, we'll lock your door."

Miss Scott reached the door without exactly walking backward but without turning her back to Lucille. She hooked the door open and stepped into the hall.

Mrs. Hammond was standing just outside, her arms folded across her flat chest. She was a handsome young woman with thick black hair and somber brown eyes, but her skin was yellowish and stretched taut over the bones of her face. She wore a black skirt and a heavy red sweater.

"Give me more food and more clotherings."

"A little quieter, please, Mrs. Hammond," Miss Scott said. "We have a new guest today. Tell Miss Parsons to give you an apple."

Miss Parsons herself appeared in the corridor. She was younger than Miss Scott and less sure of herself.

"Well, she's already had two apples and a banana, Miss Scott."

"Goodness," Miss Scott said. "You don't want to get a pain in your tummy, Mrs. Hammond."

"Give me more food . . ."

"I could give her a milk shake," Miss Parsons said nervously.

"There," Miss Scott said cheerfully, "if you're good and behave yourself Miss Parsons will give you a milk shake. You go back to your room, Mrs. Hammond. Rest period isn't over yet."

Majestically, Mrs. Hammond went down the corridor and disappeared into her room.

"Where does she put it?" Miss Parsons said in a worn voice. "Where *does* she *put* it?"

"Go down for Miss Cora. She's in the library." She lowered her voice. "I don't think Mrs. Morrow is going to be any trouble at all, except that Dr. Goodrich wants everything she says put on her chart."

Miss Parsons looked desperate. *"Everything?"*

"It's all right. She doesn't say much. Here's the key to get Miss Cora."

Miss Scott returned to her desk. It was in the center of the short corridor and from it she had a view of the open door of each room and the locked door that led to the incline.

She looked at her watch. Two-forty. That left her twenty minutes to introduce Miss Cora to her new roommate, get the ward ready for their walk and persuade Mrs. Morrow to leave her room, peacefully, and see Dr. Goodrich in his office.

She sighed, but it wasn't from weariness. It was the contented sigh of someone who has a hundred things to do and knows she can do them well.

The incline door opened and Miss Parsons came in with Miss Cora Green.

Miss Green was a small sprightly woman in her sixties. Her black silk dress was immaculately clean and pressed and her white hair was combed in hundreds of tiny pincurls with a pink velvet bow perched on top of them. She moved quickly and delicately as a bird.

"Is she here?" Miss Cora said.

"Is *who* here?" Miss Scott said, quite severely. She had to be severe with Miss Cora in order not to laugh. Miss Cora was so sharp, she knew almost as much about the patients as Dr. Goodrich, and she was continually trying to wheedle more information from the nurses.

"You *always* send me to the library when I'm getting someone new in my room," Miss Cora said. "What's the matter with her? What's her name?"

"Mrs. Morrow," Miss Scott said. "Come along and make a good impression."

"Well, the *least* you could do is to tell me what's the matter with her."

Miss Parsons and Miss Scott exchanged faint smiles.

"I don't know," Miss Scott said.

"Well the least you could do is tell me how *bad* she is. Is she as bad as Mrs. Hammond?"

"No."

"Thank heaven! I find Mrs. Hammond a *dull* woman. If I were the superintendent I'd feed her and feed her and feed her, just to see what happens. I wonder how much she could *really* eat."

Miss Scott, who had wondered the same thing herself, looked pleasantly blank. She took Miss Cora's arm and they went together into the room.

"Here is Miss Green, Mrs. Morrow."

"Miss Green?" Lucille looked up. The fear that had sprung into her eyes slid away slowly. "Miss Green?" A tiny old woman, no threat, no danger. "How do you do, Miss Green?"

"How do you do, Mrs. Morrow?" Miss Cora said. "What perfectly beautiful hair you have!" She glanced back at Miss Scott with a sly smile that said: that's the kind of thing *you* say but you're not fooling *me*.

Miss Scott pretended not to notice. "It is

lovely, isn't it? Such a pretty color. I'm sure you and Miss Green will get along splendidly, Mrs. Morrow. I'll be right out in the corridor if you want me for anything. You remember my name?"

"Miss Scott," Lucille said.

"That's fine," Miss Scott said, sounding very very pleased. She went out.

"She says a lot of silly things," Miss Cora said "They're *trained* to say silly things."

"Are they?" Lucille said.

"They underestimate our intelligence, especially mine." She studied Lucille for a minute and added pensively, "Perhaps yours too. Is there anything special the matter with you?"

"I don't know." She had felt cold and detached before, but now she had a sudden wild desire to talk, to explain herself to Miss Green: there is nothing the matter with me. I am afraid, but it is a real fear, I didn't imagine it. I am afraid I am going to be killed. I am going to be killed by one of them. Andrew, Polly, Martin, Edith, Giles, one of them.

She whispered, "I came here to be safe."

"Are people after you?"

"Yes."

"Oh, dear, they all say that," Miss Cora said, disappointed. "You mustn't tell that to

Dr. Goodrich, you'll simply *never* get out of here. They have such *suspicious* minds around this place."

Miss Scott stuck her head in the door. "Get your coat on, Cora. Time for a walk."

"I am not going for a walk today," Miss Cora stated firmly.

"Come on, that's a good girl."

"No, my neuritis is bothering me this afternoon."

"You haven't been outside for a week," Miss Scott said. While it was impossible for Miss Cora to prove she had neuritis it was equally impossible for anyone to disprove it. Miss Cora's neuritis was hard to pin down. It skipped agilely from limb to limb, it settled in the legs if a walk was necessary, in the arms if Miss Cora didn't feel like doing occupational therapy, and in the head under any provocation.

"There is also," Miss Cora pointed out, "my weak heart."

"Nonsense," Miss Scott said brusquely. "Gentle exercise is good for heart patients."

"Not for me."

Miss Scott retreated without further argument.

"The walks are very boring," Miss Cora explained to Lucille. "They do very naive things like gather leaves. The level of sophistication in this place is very low."

Miss Scott appeared again, a navy-blue cape flung over her uniform. "Good-bye, Cora. You'll be sorry you didn't come. We're going to build a lovely snow man."

"Isn't she *absurd?*" Miss Cora cried, shaking her head. "A lovely snow man. Really!"

Mrs. Hammond strode past the door muffled in an immense fur coat, with a woollen scarf tied around her head. Behind her came two stout middle-aged women who looked and were dressed exactly alike. They walked arm in arm, and in step.

"The Filsinger twins," Miss Cora said, without bothering to lower her voice. "I can't tell which is which any more. A while ago you could tell which was Mary because she was crazier. Now Betty's as bad as she is."

Miss Cora waved her hand at them and the twins disappeared, scowling.

"Mary was in here first," Miss Cora explained. "Betty used to come to see her, and was all right till a few months ago when she began to copy Mary's symptoms. Now they're both here. Mary looks after Betty, she even gives her baths." Miss Cora sighed. "It's all very Freudian. I have a sister myself but the mere thought of giving her a bath is abhorrent to me. She's quite stout, and rather hairy."

She paused, looking down at her own white delicate hands. Her movements were a little too brisk and her talking a little too fast for a woman of her age. But Lucille felt that here, of all the people she had known, was one who was entirely sane.

"I know what you're thinking," Cora said, "and of course you're quite right. I am far too sensible to cope with a nonsensical world. I'd rather stay here." She laughed. "I in my small corner and you in yours."

Somewhere in the building a gong began to ring. In a sudden panic Lucille started out of the chair but even before she was on her feet the gong had stopped again.

"That's Mary Filsinger," Cora said wryly. "Every time she goes out for a walk she runs to the fence and touches it to see if the escape alarm is still working. She never misses."

"Why?" Lucille said.

"Why? No one ever asks *why* at Penwood, it's too futile. Concentrate, instead, on the beautiful consistency and order of things — Mary Filsinger and the fence, Mrs. Hammond and her solitary sentence. There's a pattern of divine illogic about it, and the pattern doesn't change. It's what I miss in the real world, some kind of pattern that doesn't change."

"The fence," Lucille said. "If someone tried to get in here — the alarm would ring?"

"To get *in?*" Cora's voice was sharp with disappointment. She had wanted to go on talking about patterns. She had felt that she had at last acquired a roommate capable of appreciating her, a woman, like herself, who could observe life but was utterly bewildered in the living of it. "Who on earth wants to get into Penwood? The more common desire is to get out."

"I want to stay here," Lucille whispered.

"Hush." Cora jerked her head around toward the open door. "Miss Scott will be coming back in a minute. Don't let her hear you. Why do you want to stay here?"

"I don't know — I'm — afraid . . ." She felt the words pressing on her throat like bubbles ready to break. *If I told someone, I could get help, someone might help me . . . Help me, Cora. . . .*

Then she saw Cora's eyes, bright with a wild unreasonable excitement. She shrank back in the chair, pressing her fists against her breasts.

"Don't say anything," Cora said "If you want to stay here don't tell Dr Goodrich anything. Don't answer him at all, not a word. Even one word might give you away."

"Give me — away?"

"You don't belong here. But if you want to stay that's your business. Don't tell Dr. Goodrich *anything*."

"Good afternoon, Mrs. Morrow."

(Don't answer him at all.)

"I hope you're settled comfortably in your room. Sit down here, please. You may go, Miss Scott."

(Silence. Eyes. Surely he had more than two eyes?)

"Please sit down, Mrs. Morrow."

(Should I sit down? Would that be giving myself away?)

"That's better, that's fine. Perhaps you'd like a cigarette. I'm sorry we can't allow smoking in the rooms, you can understand why."

(Of course. We're children, you can't trust us with fire.)

"Can't you?"

(What is he holding out to me? A cigarette? No, a pen. Why a pen?)

"I have a few routine questions to ask you. If you'll take the pen and sign your name right here . . . What is your full name, please?. . . . What date is this anyway?"

(December 9th, but I won't tell you, you can't catch me.)

"Your full name?"

(Can't catch me.)

"What year were you born? Do you know where you are? Can you see this? Can you hear this? What color is your dress?"

The questions continued. Lucille said nothing. Dr. Goodrich was entirely unperturbed at her silence. He seemed intent on what he was writing and barely looked at her any more.

She felt secure in her silence, and suddenly triumphant. It was easy, after all, it was the easiest thing in the world to fool him. Almost boldly she glanced across the desk to see what he was writing. She saw with a shock that he wasn't writing anything; he was drawing pictures, and he'd been waiting for her to find it out, deliberately.

In that instant he looked up and their eyes met. His were kindly but a little cynical. *You're not putting anything over on me,* they said.

"All right, Mrs. Morrow," he said pleasantly. "We don't want to overdo things the first day. Miss Scott will show you back to your room."

Through a haze she saw Miss Scott

gliding across the room toward her. She put out her hands, blindly, to clutch at something safe.

Miss Scott caught her as she fell.

"She's fainted," Miss Scott said in a surprised voice.

"Put her on the couch and get a stretcher. Don't send her to the dining room tonight for dinner unless she asks to go. And send Miss Green down here, please."

Fifteen minutes later Cora arrived, flanked by a blushing Miss Parsons.

"Why on earth you have to have *her* bring me is more than I can say," Cora said. "I know my way around this place better than *she* does. And it isn't as if I'd try to escape."

Miss Parsons made a hurried exit. Cora bounced across the room toward Dr. Goodrich.

"That's what I wanted to talk to you about, Cora," Goodrich said with a faint smile.

Cora sat down. She was breathing heavily and her lips had a bluish tinge that Goodrich noted with concern.

"How do you feel, Cora?"

"Fine."

"You should learn to move more slowly."

"I've never been cautious," Cora said with

a toss of her head. "It's too late to learn now."

"Tomorrow's visitors' day. Your sister is coming. I thought it would be a good idea for you to be all packed ready to go home with her."

She stared at him. "Did you tell Janet?"

"She suggested it herself. You haven't been home for quite a while."

"I don't want to go. I'm too old to be shunted back and forth like this all the time."

"You may come back whenever you feel like it. You're much better than you were."

"You know that's a lie, doctor," Cora said. "Why do you want me to go home? Because I'm not going to last much longer, is that it?"

"Nonsense. Your sister thought you might like to come. It's up to you. If you'd rather stay here, well, you know we like to have you."

It was true. Miss Green was the favorite of the hospital. It was difficult to imagine this bright cheerful little woman getting wildly drunk whenever the opportunity presented itself. On these occasions her moral barriers were all swept away. Twice she had been arrested for stealing, and several times for disorderly conduct. Usually she remembered nothing of what she had done. After the second offense, her sister Janet had sent her to Penwood and from here she made periodic visits home. But they were not successful. Under the vigilant and worried eye of her sister, Cora felt far more irresponsible and restless than she did at Penwood. After a few days of this constant watching Cora felt impelled to escape from it. She had the subtle cunning of the superior drunkard, and Janet, an unimaginative and successful business woman, was no match for her. Cora always managed to get out, to get money, to get drunk. Her heart made these excursions increasingly dangerous.

"You know what would happen," Cora said. "You know very well I'm not cured."

Goodrich, who knew it very well, said nothing.

"How many of us *ever* are?" she demanded.

"Not many."

"I used to think that once I knew *why* I drank I could stop, just like that." She snapped her fingers. "But nothing is so simple as it seems. I know, and you know, why I drink."

He let her talk, though he knew her history in every detail. She had been fifteen when both her parents died, leaving her with a five-year-old sister to look after. For twenty-five years she had done her job thoroughly and unselfishly. As Janet began to succeed in business Cora began to go downhill. Her memory often failed her and she became almost scatterbrained in dealing with situations and people. She was throwing off the weight of a responsibility that had been too heavy for her. Now, though the weight was gone, the mind remembered, guiltily, the feel and contours of it.

"The responsibility is still there," Cora said. "It will be there until I die. . . . Oh, Lord, I'm getting heavy, aren't I? I don't like heavy people."

She rose, pulling herself up by clinging to the arms of the chair.

Goodrich noticed. "Better drop in on Dr. Laverne for a checkup tomorrow, Cora."

"I don't need a checkup. I feel fine."

"I'll arrange it."

"All this silly fussing," Cora said. "It would hardly be a tragedy for an old woman of sixty to die."

"Don't cheat, Cora. Sixty-six."

She turned away, laughing. "All the less of a tragedy."

Cora Green died two days later.

During the week the Morrow family visited Lucille, a small boy called Maguire found a parcel washed up on the beach and took it home to his mother. And on the same day an inquest was held on the body of Eddy Greeley.

CHAPTER 7

Both in life and in death Mr. Greeley was a public nuisance. Alive, he had cost the province his board and room for several years, and by dying in an alley he was responsible for the cost of an inquest and the loss of the valuable time of the coroner, the jury and the police surgeon.

Edwin Edward Greeley, the police surgeon stated, was a morphine addict of long standing. The body was in an emaciated condition and both thighs had hundreds of hypodermic scars and several infected punctures. Examination of Mr. Greeley's trousers (not on exhibit) showed that he was in the habit of injecting the morphine through his clothing with a home-made syringe (exhibited to the jury who eyed it with interest and disgust).

An autopsy proved the cause of death to be morphine poisoning.

The coroner went over the evidence, implying strongly that he himself had no doubt that Greeley had miscalculated and given himself an overdose (and no loss to the world, his tone made clear); however, if the jury wanted to make fools of themselves they were perfectly welcome to do so and bring in a verdict of homicide or suicide.

The jury was out twenty minutes. Miss Alicia Schaefer summed up the opinions of the other jurors when she stated that anybody who would use a syringe like that instead of going out and buying a proper one, and using it through his clothes, imagine!, instead of having it properly sterilized, well, anybody like that could make any kind of mistake.

Miss Schaefer's compelling logic carried the day, and it became part of the court records that Edwin Edward Greeley had died by misadventure.

The bartender at the Allen Hotel read the news in the *Evening Telegram.* He called Inspector Sands' office and left a message for him.

Shortly after seven o'clock on Thursday night Sands came in and sat in the back booth and ordered a beer.

"You wanted to see me?" he said to Bill.

"Yeah," Bill said. "I see by the papers that Greeley got his."

"Friend of yours?"

"Not so's you'd notice. He was in here couple nights ago. Must have been the night he conked. Tuesday."

"Well?"

"He had a tart from down the street with him. He ordered champagne and paid for it with a fifty."

Sands didn't look impressed, and Bill added anxiously, "I guess maybe that don't sound like much, but I had a kind of idea he was onto something big. He shot off at the mouth about how from now on he's got a steady income. I figured you'd like to know."

"Thanks."

"Jesus, he's got a steady income now, all right. Laying gold bricks."

"Who was the hooker?"

"Susie. She's from Phyllis's house down the street, a big redhead. Nice girl. I figure there's nothing against her. Maybe she gets a case now and then but she ain't mean."

"Does she come in here often?"

"Now and then."

"I'd like to talk to her. How would you like to dig her up for me?"

"Aw, now, Mr. Sands," Bill said. "What the hell. I got a wife and family. I don't whore, you know that. If my wife'd hear about it . . ."

"Use a phone."

"Sure. I never thought of that. Why, sure,

Mr. Sands." He got up. "It'll probably cost you some money. I figure I'll say it's a business appointment."

"Good idea."

"You got five bucks to waste?"

"Yes."

Bill went into the office. After assuring the manager of the house that he meant business, five bucks' worth, he was allowed to speak to Susie.

"Susie? This is Bill, up at the Allen."

"Well, what do you want? Or is that too personal?"

"There's a guy here. Five bucks."

"I don't want to come out on a stinking night like this for five bucks."

"You see in the papers about Greeley? He got his wings. And I don't mean the kind that lets you fly a plane."

"Well, well," Susie said thoughtfully and hung up.

Fifteen minutes later she was at the Allen. She had dressed in a hurry and hadn't combed her hair and her lipstick was blurred around her mouth.

Bill took her to the back booth and introduced her to Sands. She looked Sands up and down very slowly.

"Who are you kidding?" she said.

"Jesus, you can't talk to Mr. Sands like

that," Bill said. "Why, Mr. Sands . . ."

"Sit down, Susie," Sands said. "You're right, I'm harmless."

"I didn't mean that," Susie said. "Holy God, I wouldn't say a thing like that to any guy. I meant, you're not the type."

"How do you know?" Bill said, scowling. "Mr. Sands has a hell of a lot of muscle under those clothes, ain't you, Mr. Sands?"

"Blow," Sands said, without looking at him.

"Sure," Bill said. "Sure. I'm on my way."

When he had gone Susie sat down. "What's the gag?"

"Questions. About Greeley."

"I get it. Policeman?"

"Yes."

Surprisingly, she leaned back and smiled. "That's a relief. I'm kind of tired tonight. And I got nothing on my conscience you don't know about."

"Known Greeley long?"

"Not so long. Two months maybe, just in the line of business. He was a cheapskate. You could have knocked me over with a feather when he came in Tuesday night and paid ten bucks for the whole night and didn't even stay. We came here and stayed for a couple of hours and guess what we drank."

"Champagne," Sands said.

"Yeah, can you beat it? Poor Eddy, it must have been too much for his system. Bill told me he died."

"Yes."

"Did you know him?"

"Not personally."

"He was a hophead. He gave himself a dose after we left the pier."

"What time?"

"Twelve, or so."

"And then?"

"Then he sent me home in a taxi," Susie said dryly. "Believe it or not. He said he had to meet someone. He'd been talking big stuff all night. It made me laugh. The only thing Eddy was good for was rolling drunks, like he must have done to get that fifty."

Sands gave her five dollars. She took it with a wry smile.

"Easy money. Wish to hell I could always get paid for talking. You couldn't see me for mink."

Sands got up and put on his hat. "Good night, and thanks."

"Too bad you got to go."

"Yes. I have an appointment."

He didn't mention that the appointment was at the morgue, with the mortal remains of Mr. Greeley. Nobody had claimed

Greeley and he was due for a long cold wait before someone did.

The morgue attendant slid out the slab like a drawer out of a filing cabinet.

"You want me to stick around, Inspector?"

"No," Sands said. His face looked gray and when he reached out to take the sheet off Greeley his hands were shaking.

The morgue was intensely quiet. None of the street sounds penetrated the walls and the harsh white ceiling lights emphasized the silence. Light should have motion and sound to go with it, but there was no motion except the fall of the sheet and no sound but Sands' own breathing.

Mercilessly the lights stared down at Greeley like cold impartial eyes, examining the protruding bones, the misshapen feet, the broken grimy toenails, the legs skinny and hairy and slightly bowed. Whoever had washed Greeley had done a poor job, and whoever had stuffed his chest with sawdust and sewed him up after the autopsy had been equally careless.

Greeley, a nuisance from first to last, and even yet a nuisance for nobody wanted to pay for his burial.

"Greeley," Sands said.

It was the only epitaph Greeley got and he

wouldn't have liked it if he'd known it came from a policeman.

Sands bent over, forcing himself to touch the cold flesh.

Later he telephoned Dr. Dutton, one of the coroner's assistants.

"I just had a look at Edwin Greeley," he said.

"Greeley? Oh yes. Accident case."

"Did you notice a puncture on his left upper arm?"

"Can't recall it. He was so full of punctures it's a wonder he could walk."

"This one's on his arm, barely noticeable."

"What of it? The inquest is over. The evidence was perfectly clear. It was either accident or suicide and I can't see that it makes much difference at this stage of the game. Are you thinking of *murder?*"

Sutton sounded incredulous and quite irritated. "You know me, Sands. I'm always on the lookout for homicide. There's not a chance of it in this case. I knew Greeley, had to testify that he was an addict a couple of years ago. He was a damned suspicious man. If you think he'd stand around while somebody shot a lethal dose of morphine into him . . ."

"How would he know it was lethal?"

Sands asked softly. "Here's something else for you. I just found out that Greeley took a shot of morphine around twelve Tuesday night. He was found the next morning around six, and had been dead about three hours or so, is that right?"

"Right."

"Well, think about it a minute. There's no hurry, Greeley won't run away."

There was a long silence.

"Yeah," Sutton said at last. "I catch it. The times are wrong. If the shot that killed him was the one he took at twelve, he didn't die soon enough. So it wasn't the twelve o'clock one."

"And carrying the time element further," Sands said, "why would Greeley take another dose some two hours later? Addicts don't throw the stuff around. Greeley had an appointment some time after twelve. It looks as though he hopped himself up for it, and then someone gave him a little extra."

The case of Mr. Greeley was unofficially re-opened on Friday morning.

On Friday morning, too, Dr. Goodrich made his second report to Andrew by phone.

"It's difficult for me to give you any definite statement at this stage," Goodrich said.

"As a gynecologist you've had plenty of experience with the mental disturbances of women during the menopause period. Usually the disturbances are fairly light — insomnia, bad dreams with a latent sexual content, periods of hysteria or depression . . ."

"You think that's what's the matter with her?" Andrew said.

"Frankly, I don't. It's intensified the situation, of course. But she seems to be suffering the after-effects of a very severe shock. She is dazed and badly frightened, so frightened that I get the impression that she wants to stay here because it is safe. That's not uncommon, we have quite a few patients here who refuse to leave, but they're ones who've been here for a long time and who can't bring themselves to give up their changeless routine and face a changing world again. But your wife is a newcomer; they usually fight to get out. . . . Are you sure you've been entirely frank with me about the preceding events?"

"I've told you everything I know," Andrew said, listlessly. "She was alone in the house with the two maids and a man delivered a parcel. No one knows what was in it. She took it with her when she left."

"There was no difficulty between the two

of you? At Mrs. Morrow's age, sometimes . . ."

"No difficulty at all. We've been married fifteen years and Lucille has been the best possible wife. And I — I don't know what kind of husband I've been, but she seemed happy." He paused and added quietly, "Very happy, I think."

"This fear of hers," Goodrich said. "It's not thc wild irrational type we find here so often. I was wondering if it might do any good to have you and the rest of your family come here this afternoon. Some frank talking might clear the air somewhat. On the other hand, you understand it might do some harm?"

"I understand. Will she — will she want to see us?"

"We might have a little trouble there, but so far she's been co-operative about doing things and she can probably be persuaded."

"Of course we'll come. We want to do everything possible to help her."

"Her difficulty seems to have started with that parcel. I'd like to know what was in it. I haven't asked her, naturally, since she has refused to answer even my ordinary questions. But my own idea is that it was some token from the past, and that, coming when it did, it's caused some exaggerated guilt complex."

"We'll do everything we can," Andrew said. "We — feel it very keenly. My daughter was to have been married this afternoon."

"What a pity," Goodrich said. "Three o'clock would be the best time. I'll see you then."

The taxi came up the driveway and Giles leaned over and picked up his suitcase.

"Well, good-bye, Giles," Polly said. "Nice to have known you."

"Oh, for God's sake." He let the suitcase fall again. It sent up a little cloud of snow as it landed. "Are we going into it right from the beginning again?"

"I don't like people who run out on things."

"I'm not running very far. To the Ford Hotel, in strict fact. I can't stay here any longer, I'm in the way and you know it."

"You've changed quite a bit in the last few days." She scuffed the snow with the toe of her shoe, scowling at it. "You didn't used to be rude *all* of the time."

"I can't stay here," he repeated. "I feel like the worst kind of fool. The expectant bridegroom out on a limb and the fire department out to lunch." He looked down at her, helplessly. "Damn it, you shouldn't stand out here without a coat."

The taxi driver honked the horn.

"You'd better hurry," Polly said flatly.

"Polly, I'll phone you when I get there."

She looked at him coldly. "What for?"

He leaned down to kiss her but she turned her head away. He put his hands on her shoulders and swung her around again.

"Look," he said. "You've made a mistake about me. I'm not a man like your father."

"Leave my father out of this. He's a better man than you'll ever be."

"That's what I'm saying," he told her quietly. "He's big enough not to resent being bossed around by the women in his family. But I can't take it like that. If I could I'd make my peace and agree to stay here and take whatever comes. You can't have it *all* your own way, Polly."

"Can't I?"

He picked up his suitcase again. "You know where I am if you want me."

"Certainly."

She turned and walked toward the house without looking back. With a savage bewildered, "Damn," he strode to the taxi and opened the door.

Slowly Polly went into the living room

and stared for a minute, her eyes hot with rage, at the small photograph of Lucille on the mantle.

"She did it," she said through clenched teeth. "She did it, it's her fault. She's always spoiled everything for me."

The occupational-therapy department consisted of two large cheerful rooms with wide windows through which the sun was pouring. There were two nurses in the room as well as the teacher, but they wore bright-colored smocks over their uniforms and the place had the atmosphere of a friendly informal workshop.

In one corner fibers of willow-wood were soaking in a tub of water and standing beside the tub was Mrs. Hammond weaving the wood on an upright frame. She paid little attention to detail but seemed to enjoy flipping the strands violently around.

"Come, come, Mrs. Hammond," the teacher said. "Let's take it a little more slowly." She turned to Lucille. "Mrs. Hammond is making a lampstand. Isn't she doing well?"

"Yes," Lucille said.

Mrs. Hammond went on flipping.

"If you see anything you'd especially care to work at, Mrs. Morrow . . ."

"No. No — anything — anything at all."

"Come, Cora," the teacher called across the room. "Let's get to work now. Show Mrs. Morrow your lovely picture. Perhaps she'd like to do one like it."

"I'm sure she would," Cora said primly.

Cora had a small niche of her own occupied by a wooden frame with a piece of burlap stretched across it. On a table beside it lay little bowls of macaroni, barley, rice and similar foods.

"We glue these to the burlap," the teacher said to Lucille. "And when the whole thing is done, it is painted. Some of the work is really amazing, though Cora, I'm afraid, is not very diligent."

"It isn't diligence that counts," Cora said with a wink. "It's the artistic impulse, and scope."

"It certainly has a great deal of scope," the teacher said and glanced at the odd pieces of rice and barley scattered haphazard over the frame. "I'm still not *quite* sure what it's going to be."

"It's a pictorial representation of James Joyce's *Ulysses*. I believe I told you that before. The medium is perfect for the work."

The teacher hesitated. "Well, in that case . . . Would you care to do something along this line, Mrs. Morrow?"

"She could work on this with me," Cora said.

"Let Mrs. Morrow answer for herself, Cora. We must be polite."

"All right," Lucille said. "I don't care."

Mrs. Hammond had stopped work and was staring at the bowls of food with somber eyes. Unobtrusively, one of the nurses moved across the room and stood beside her.

"Give me more food and more clotherings," Mrs. Hammond intoned. "Give me . . ."

"Now, Mrs. Hammond, you've just had your breakfast. We'll give you a little lunch later on. What a really good job you're . . ."

". . . more food and more clotherings."

The nurse picked up a strand of willow and handed it to her. Mrs. Hammond flung it down again. It whistled through the air and struck the nurse's leg.

"Give me more food and more clotherings."

"All right. Come along."

The two went out, the nurse's arm tucked inside Mrs. Hammond's in a firm friendly way.

"She's always worse on visitors' day," Cora explained. "Her husband comes to see her. Here, pretend you're working and the teacher won't interrupt us talking."

Lucille selected a piece of macaroni from the bowl. She held it up between her fingers and gazed at it dully. It seemed to expand before her eyes, to become the symbol of her future life.

All of my life, she thought, all of my life, while Cora's voice tinkled on: "Mrs. Hammond came from a very wealthy Jewish family. Then she married this man, a clerk of some kind, and her family cut her off because he wasn't Jewish. They were very poor, and then she lost her baby at birth. Since they told her she's never said a word but that one sentence. On visitors' day her husband comes and talks to her, but I don't think she hears anything. She's been here for a long time."

A long time? Lucille thought. So will I.

"You aren't listening," Cora said.

"Yes, I am."

"Well, then, Mrs. Hammond must feel that her husband starved her and killed the baby. And at the same time she must blame herself too, for renouncing her religion."

The Filsinger twins came in with Miss Scott. Mary identified herself immediately.

"I have told the superintendent a thousand times that when Betty doesn't feel well she shouldn't have to come down here." She threw back her head and shouted, "Superintendent. Super — in — ten — dent!"

"Hush, Mary," Miss Scott said, and turned to Betty. "How do you feel, Betty?"

"I feel fine," Betty said vacantly.

"She's putting on a brave front!" Mary cried. "She doesn't look well — oh, any simpleton could see how pale she is."

She stroked her sister's rosy cheek.

The teacher appeared from the other room.

"Mary, Miss Sims is going to have her washrag finished before you if you don't hurry. She's tatting the edge right this minute."

Mary snorted. "Come on, Betty, come on, Betty. Watch you don't fall. Oh, you shouldn't be allowed to come down here in your condition. Don't fall, Betty."

"I feel fine," Betty said.

"Oh, you're so brave, dear. If it wasn't for Miss Sims beating me, I'd go right to the superintendent this minute. Oh, dear. Oh, Miss Scott, am I doing right?"

"Perfectly right," Miss Scott said.

The morning went on. Except for Mary Filsinger's occasional cries for the superintendent, there were no disturbances. Lucille and Cora were skillfully separated by the teacher and Lucille found herself becoming genuinely interested in Mrs. Hammond's abandoned lampstand. She liked the feel of the willow fibers, smooth and pliant, and for the first time in years she felt the satisfaction of actually constructing something with her hands. When the luncheon bell sounded she had almost forgotten where she was and that she was to stay there the rest of her life.

"I won't go down." Lucille stood by the window in her room, her hands clenched against her sides. "I don't want to see anyone."

"Oh, come now," Miss Scott said. "We all have visitors today, even the twins. You'll be all alone up here. And after your family sent you those lovely roses . . ."

"I don't want the roses. Give them to someone else."

She had never dreamt that the family would come to see her, openly and casually like this. She had imagined one of them sneaking in, in the dead of night, to find her, to make her suffer. Yet they were here now, all of them, waiting downstairs to see her as if nothing had happened, sending her roses, and pretending this was an ordinary hospital and she herself was merely a little ill.

"We know it's always hard to see your

family for the first time," Miss Scott said, "but if you could make the effort we feel it will do you worlds of good."

"Like Mrs. Hammond," Lucille said.

Miss Scott looked almost cross for a moment. "Cora does a great deal too much talking. You want to see your husband, don't you?"

Lucille pressed her hands to her heart. *I want to see Andrew, to go home with him, to live with him all of my life, never even bothering to see anyone else.*

"No, I don't," she said.

"Very well, I'll tell Dr. Goodrich. You may stay up here."

When she had gone Lucille sat down on the edge of the bed. She was barely conscious. Though her body was upright and her eyes open, it was as if she was almost asleep and her mind in labor and heaving with dreams, little faces, willow fingers, roses of blood, clotherings and a pellet of rice, did you count the spoons, nurse?, hard dead flesh of macaroni, doing as well as can be expected, are those roses for me, for *me,* for *me?*

Willow drowned in a tub. Soft dead willow floating hair and headache in a tub.

Superintendent!

How smooth how dear, how dear. Come

Cora Cora, come Cora.

Super — in — ten — dent!

Grape eyes mashed, rotten nose splashed on a wall, I'm sure you'll love the soup today, it floats the willow, nursie, nursie . . .

Suddenly she leaned over and began to retch.

Miss Scott came running. "Mrs. Morrow! Here. Head down. Head down, please."

She pressed Lucille's head down against her knees and held it. "Breathe deeply, that's right, that's better. We'll be fine again in a minute. It must have been something you ate."

Miss Scott took her hands away, and slowly Lucille raised her head. She knew Miss Scott was there, she could see her and hear her, but Miss Scott wasn't really there, she was a cloud of white smoke, you could wave her away with your hands, blow her away, she didn't matter, she couldn't do anything, she wasn't there.

"Would you like a glass of water, Mrs. Morrow? Here, let me wipe your mouth, you've bitten your lip. There now do we feel better?"

(Didums bitums ittle ip?)

"There, drink this. I'm sure you're upset because you didn't go down to see your family. They're awfully worried about you,

you know. You wouldn't want to upset them, would you now?"

Miss Scott expected no answer. She went to the dresser and picked up a comb and began to comb Lucille's hair. Then she brushed off Lucille's dress and straightened the belt. Passive, indifferent, Lucille allowed herself to be guided through the door.

"We felt it was better for you to meet your family in Dr. Goodrich's office, not in the common room. Here we are. Would you like to go in alone?"

Lucille shook her head. She meant to shake it just once, but she couldn't seem to stop, she felt her head shaking and shaking. Briskly, Miss Scott reached up and steadied it.

The door opened and Dr. Goodrich came out into the corridor. Miss Scott frowned at him and tipped her head almost imperceptibly toward Lucille.

"I see," he said. "Come in, Mrs. Morrow. Here is your family."

Andrew came over to her and kissed her cheek. The others sat stiffly on the leather couch, as if they didn't know what was expected of them.

Then Edith, too, rose and came toward her.

"Lucille, dear," she said, and their cheeks

touched for an instant in the old familiar gesture.

Lucille stood, rubbing and rubbing her cheek.

(Here is your family. At least they *said* it was your family, and there was some faint resemblance to Andrew in the tall man. But the girl, who was she? And the young man? And the scraggly hag who'd kissed her? Ho, ho, ho, ho. What a joke! But she knew.)

"Hello, Lucille."

"It's nice to see you again, Lucille."

"Hello, Lucille. I like your hair-do."

"Will you sit down, Mrs. Morrow?"

"We've been so worried about you, Lucille, not letting us know or anything . . ."

(That was the hag who wasn't Edith. Her voice was Edith's, high, piercing, thin as a wire, but Edith had never looked like this, a dried and shriveled mummy with sick-yellow skin. Yet — yet . . .)

"Edith?" she said, her face wrinkling in pain and bewilderment. "Is that you, Edith?" She looked slowly around the room. "And you, Andrew? And you, Polly — Martin . . . ? This is a surprise. I didn't know you were coming."

(There was something wrong about that, but it wasn't important, she would figure it out later.)

"This *is* a surprise. I feel so confused."

Andrew brought her a chair, and when she sat down he stood beside her, his hand on her shoulder, strong and steady.

"If you have any troubles, Lucille," he said gently, "share them with us. That's what a family is for."

"So confused — and tired."

"You can trust us, darling. Whatever is bothering you, it's probably not nearly as bad as you think it is." He looked over at Polly and Martin. "Tell her, tell her, Polly, Martin, tell her we're all behind her, whatever . . ."

"Of course," Polly said stiffly. "Of course. Lucille knows that."

"Sure," Martin said, but he didn't look across the room at her.

"If you'd tell us what happened," Edith said shrilly. "There's been so much mystery. I'm worried half to death. What did the man . . . ?"

"I'm so tired," Lucille said. "I'm sure you'll excuse me."

She moved slightly.

"Please!" Andrew said and tightened his grip on her shoulder. "Please!"

With a sudden cry she wrenched herself out of his grasp and ran to the door. An instant later Dr. Goodrich was in the corridor beside her.

Edith clung to Andrew. Her body was shaking with silent sobs and her hands clawed desperately at his coat sleeve. "Take me home, Andrew, please take me home, I'm frightened! She is — she really is *crazy!* I'll be like that some day, I know it, she's just my age. . . ."

"Behave yourself," Andrew said, and looked down at her with an ugly smile. "People with as little sense as you have rarely lost it. Law of compensation, Edith."

Martin was lighting a cigarette. He seemed absorbed in the flare of the match, as if by watching it he could learn something vital.

"I hate to be wise after the fact," he said, "but I think we've underestimated Lucille. We shouldn't have come. She knows that Polly and I have never been friendly to her. It's not anybody's fault, it just happened like that. If she ran away from the lot of us on Monday what reason had we for thinking she was going to break down and confess all on Friday?"

He glanced over at Polly who was staring sulkily down at the floor. "Certainly the sight of Polly's sunny little face isn't going to do anyone any good."

"Take a look at your own," Polly said.

"I have. I grant it doesn't measure up. Still, I try. A for effort."

"Oh, it's so terrible!" Edith cried. "There they are wrangling again as if — as if they didn't care where they were — and poor Lucille — she doesn't *matter* to them!"

"She matters a great deal," Polly said with a dry little smile. "Or haven't you noticed? She matters so much that I wasn't married today, that my fiancé couldn't even stay in the same house with me. . . . She's managed to mess things up very nicely for me."

"Don't be mawkish," Martin said. "Giles was polite enough to leave until things were settled."

"Sure." Polly shrugged. "Very polite of him."

"You sound like the deserted bride."

"How should I sound? He might have stood by me for a while until . . ."

Martin's voice sliced her sentence. "Since when are you the type that asks to be stood by? Or even wants it?"

"Stop it!" Edith said. "Stop your wrangling. It's indecent."

Dr. Goodrich returned to the room.

"I'm sorry," he said. "I thought it was advisable for Mrs. Morrow to go to her room. She seems far more irrational this afternoon than she did this morning." He glanced, with sympathy, at Andrew. "I'm sorry things didn't work out better. But there is a good deal of trial and error in these cases, it's the only way we learn. In its present stage psychiatry has many classifications and rules, but far more exceptions. What I am trying to tell you is not to expect results too soon."

"I see," Andrew said slowly.

"And for the present I think your wife should have no visitors."

"I'm not to come again?"

"I'll let you know when I think it's advisable. Meanwhile it would be a good idea to send her gifts, flowers and fruit and little things. She must be given the feeling that her family care for her and are thinking of her."

"We are," Polly said. "We think of very little else."

Odd girl, Dr. Goodrich thought fleetingly. He shook hands with Andrew. "By the way, Dr. Morrow, if you're driving back to town, perhaps you'd give a lift to someone here."

"Certainly."

"He's had a bad time. His — one of his relatives is here and became disturbed. His face is scratched. I'd like to feel he'll get home all right."

"We'll be glad to take him."

In the corridor a nurse was standing talking to a thin shabby man. The man had his hands in his pockets, and his head was bent over as if he was too tired to hold it up any longer.

"Mr. Hammond," Dr. Goodrich said. "Dr. Morrow is going into town and will be glad to give you a lift."

Hammond raised his head. His face was very pale, the only color in it was in the red-rimmed eyes and the three long scratches down his cheek.

"Thanks," he said huskily. "Very nice of you."

He didn't look at anyone. When he walked down the corridor he moved as if his whole body was in pain.

CHAPTER 8

"There's a man and woman and kid down here," the desk sergeant told Sands on the phone. "They've got the damnedest story I ever heard. I don't know exactly where to send them."

"You have every intention of sending them up here," Sands said.

"Seems up your alley, Inspector, but I don't know."

"Send them up."

The Maguire family was escorted into Sands' office. The boy was about ten, and looked intelligent and thoroughly awed by his surroundings. He had to be prodded into the office by his mother's large competent thumb.

The Maguires looked respectable lower-middle-class, and uncertain, and the combination, Sands knew, would merge into belligerence unless he could restore their self-assurance.

"I'm sure I don't know whether I'm doing right or not," Mrs. Maguire said loudly. "I told John, I said, maybe we should just phone, or maybe we should come right down."

"Personal interviews are so much more satisfactory," Sands said. "Few people are intelligent enough to do as you've done."

It was broad, but so was Mrs. Maguire. She relaxed far enough to sit down, although giving the impression that she considered all chairs booby-traps.

"It's like this. Tommy was out playing this morning; it's Saturday and no school, and sometimes he goes down to the lake. I don't know, he just seems crazy about water, he can swim like a fish, and his father and me don't take to the water at all."

"Let me tell it," Tommy said. "Let *me* tell it."

"That's a fine way to behave in front of a policeman! You hold your tongue." Mrs. Maguire opened her purse and brought out a parcel wrapped in newspaper. She laid it on the desk, as if she was reluctant to touch it. "I put the newspaper around it myself. After I saw what was in the box I couldn't hardly bear to wrap it up again."

"You're telling it wrong," the boy said.

"Show some respect to your mother," Mr. Maguire said.

"I found it on the beach," the boy said, ignoring both his parents. "I often find things there, once fifty cents. So when I found this box I thought there'd be something in it, so I took it home."

"First, I could hardly believe my eyes," Mrs. Maguire said in an agitated voice. "I didn't even recognize what it was. It was sort of swollen, being soaked in the water and all."

Sands removed the newspaper and revealed a water-soaked cardboard box which almost fell apart under his hands. Mrs. Maguire turned her head away, but the boy watched, fascinated.

A few minutes later Sands was in Dr. Sutton's office.

"Take a look at that."

Sutton looked. "Been robbing graves?"

"What is it?"

"A finger. To be exact, a forefinger, probably male, and sliced off by an expert. The bones are badly crushed, probably had to be amputated." He grimaced. "Hell-of-a-looking thing. Take it away. The joke's over."

"It's just beginning," Sands said.

"Where did you get the thing?"

"A boy found it on the beach. I think someone flung it into the lake last Monday, but the waves washed it up. It couldn't have been in the water long, the box would have fallen apart."

"Got a corpse to fit it?"

"Not yet," Sands said. "Possibly it doesn't belong to a corpse."

"Maybe not," Sutton said. "Maybe the guy that owns it is going around looking for it."

"Your humor is nauseous stuff, Sutton."

"Can't be helped. Leave the thing here and I'll examine it in the lab."

"Don't die laughing about it, will you?" Sands said and went out of the room. He felt unjustly irritated with Sutton who was, he knew, a kind and simple young man. Perhaps too simple. To Sutton the finger was merely a finger, bones and skin, gristle and ganglia. To Sands it was part of a man, once warmed and fed by flowing blood, articulated and responsive to a living brain, knowing the feel of wind and grass, the touch of a woman.

He went back to his office and put on his hat and coat, slowly, because he dreaded the job he had to do.

Ten miles west of Toronto stand the iron gates of Penwood, protecting its inmates against the world and the world against its inmates. At the ornamental apertures in the gates society could press a cold peering eye, but inside, the little colony carried on, undisturbed and uncaring. It grew most of its own food, ran a dairy farm, handled its own laundry, and sold samples of needlework, watercolors, and wicker baskets to a curious public. ("Made by a crazy person, imagine! Why it's just as good as I could do!")

The colony was fathered by its superintendent, Dr. Nathan, a psychoanalyst turned business executive, and mothered by its host of nurses, chosen for their quality of efficient and cheerful callousness. No nurse who confessed to daydreaming, or sentimentalism, or an interest in art, was accepted on the staff. A surplus of imagination could be more dangerous than stupidity, and a weakness for emotionalism could destroy the peace of a whole ward.

Miss Scott had none of these undesirable qualities. In addition to her vital lacks she had a sense of responsibility and a detached fondness for all of her charges. Miss Scott listened and observed and because she had a poor memory she committed her observations to paper, thus doubling her value. She pitied her patients (while impersonally noting that there were lots of people worse off than they were) but when she went off duty at night she was able to forget the day entirely and devote herself to her succession of boy friends.

Incapable of a grand passion, she was the kind of woman who would one day make an advantageous marriage, stick to it, and produce curly-headed and conveniently spaced offspring.

Though he didn't admire the type, Sands liked Miss Scott at once.

"I'm Miss Scott," she said in her warm bright voice. "Dr. Goodrich is doing his rounds right now. I understand you want to see Mrs. Morrow."

"I do," Sands said. "My name is Sands, Inspector Sands."

Miss Scott gave him a well-what-do-you-inspect? glance.

"I'm a detective. Homicide. I'm afraid I have to see Mrs. Morrow."

"I'm sorry, I don't think Dr. Goodrich will allow it," Miss Scott said. "She was quite disturbed last night. She's still N.Y.D., I mean not yet diagnosed, and Dr. Goodrich . . ."

"If I could possibly get out of seeing Mrs. Morrow, I'd be glad to do it. I rarely pinch children or attack the sick, but sometimes it's necessary."

What a queer man, Miss Scott thought, and was dumbfounded into temporary silence.

"In this case it is," Sands said. "What I

have to say to Mrs. Morrow may, remotely, help her. More probably it will disturb her further. I wanted this to be clear before I see her."

"Under those conditions, I'm sure Dr. Goodrich will refuse to let you see her."

"Perhaps not." He turned his head and seemed to be contemplating the brown-leather furniture of the waiting room. But perhaps he will refuse, Sands thought, and in that case I'll have to tell him what I know. But what to tell?

The picture wasn't clear, the only real figure in it was Lucille herself haunted by dreams and driven by the devils locked up in her own heart. The rest of the picture was in shadow, blurred stealthy shapes merging into darkness, a face (Greeley's?), a finger, a hump in the snow (Mildred?).

"Well, Dr. Goodrich will be here any minute," Miss Scott said and moved toward the door, glad to return to the world of unreason where everything was, in the long run, much simpler.

She stopped at the parcel desk to pick up the gifts for her suite. Everything, even the flowers, had been opened, inspected, and done up again.

Chocolates for Cora. Flowers and a basket of fruit and a bed-jacket for Mrs.

Morrow, the morning newspaper, no longer a newspaper but merely selected items clipped and pasted on a piece of cardboard. Mrs. Hammond's daily box of food from her family. The Yiddish delicacies looked very tempting and Miss Scott had often wanted to taste some but Mrs. Hammond always grabbed the box and disappeared with it into the bathroom.

It was an unwritten rule that Cora should get the newspaper first and complain of it.

"Why I can't have a decent ordinary paper is more than I can say," Cora said.

"Now, Cora," Miss Scott said, "look at the goodies you got."

"I loathe chocolates. Will Janet never learn?"

"We're a little cross this morning, aren't we?"

"Oh, really!" Cora said, half-laughing in exasperation. "What are the other parcels?"

"For Mrs. Morrow. Here you are, Mrs. Morrow."

"Thank you," Lucille said in a frozen polite voice. "Thank you very much."

She didn't put out her hand to take the parcels, so Miss Scott herself opened them, making happy noises as she worked.

"Hm! A bed-jacket. Look, Mrs. Morrow. It matches your eyes almost exactly. We're going to look lovely in it."

"Certainly," Cora said. "You in one sleeve and Lucille in the other."

"Now, Cora," Miss Scott said in reproof.

"If I were running this place I would insist on some form of intelligent communication."

Quite unruffled, Miss Scott unwrapped the flowers, and the basket of Malaga grapes. "Shall I read the cards to you? Well, the bed-jacket is from Edith. 'Lucille dear, I know this is your favorite . . .' "

"Don't bother," Lucille said.

" '. . . color and how it becomes you. Love from Edith.' The grapes are from Polly, with love. And your husband sent the flowers. 'Remember we are all behind you, Andrew.' Aren't they sweet little mums?"

"Yes," Lucille said. Sweet little mums, little secret faces with shaggy hair drooping over them, sweet flowers, a rosebud of cancer on a breast, a blue bloated grape, drowned woman, bile-green leaves, cold, doomed, grow no more.

"Yes," Lucille said. "Thank you very much."

But Miss Scott was gone, and so was Cora. How had they gotten out without her seeing them go? She was watching and listening, wasn't she? How long ago was it?

How long had she been alone?

Her eyes fell on the flowers. The flowers, yes. She didn't like them looking at her. She may have missed Cora and Miss Scott leaving the room, but she was perfectly rational about this. The roses had squeezed-up sly little faces. You couldn't see the eyes but of course they were there. Weren't they? Look into one. Take it apart and you will find the eyes.

The torn petals fell softly as snowflakes.

"Why, Mrs. Morrow, you're not going to tear up your lovely flowers," Miss Scott said. "My goodness, I should say not."

Had she been gone and come back again? Or had she never left at all? *No, she must have left, I'm quite rational; it's perfectly sensible to look for eyes if you think they're there.*

Miss Scott was moving the flowers, taking away the rosebuds and the shaggy-haired chrysanthemum children. Miss Scott was talking. Was she saying "We mustn't tear our lovely children"? What silly things she said sometimes. As if anyone would tear a child.

"Come along, Mrs. Morrow. Miss Parsons will take you down to Dr. Goodrich's office. That's right, dear, come along."

Docile, a bruised petal still between her fingers, Lucille moved out into the hall.

Cora looked coldly across the room at Miss Scott.

"Is it possible to talk sense to you?"

"Oh, come off it, Cora," Miss Scott said. "None of that."

"I wondered."

"Talk if you want to."

"I shall," Cora said. "In the meager hope that something will get across. Mrs. Morrow is deathly afraid."

"Yes, she is, isn't she?" Miss Scott said thoughtfully.

"She's afraid of her family. She told me last night. One of them is trying to kill her."

"Oh, come, Cora. I thought you had too much sense to believe . . ."

"I believe her," Cora said.

"Don't worry your pretty head about it. She's in good hands, she's safe here, even if it's true. Come, cheer up. The superintendent will be around in a few minutes and you wouldn't want him to see you down in the dumps like this."

"Have you ever been afraid, really afraid?"

"I don't remember. Besides, why would anyone want to kill Mrs. Morrow?"

"I've been afraid," Cora said. "For Janet's sake. When the epidemic of flu was on after the last war . . ."

"Get your hair combed, dear. You look a

sight. Dr. Nathan will be disappointed in you."

Lucille knew that Sands' face was one of the thousands of little faces that pursued her with silent shrieks through dreams and half-dreams. But she could not remember where he fitted in, and even when he told her his name she merely felt, vaguely, that he was a part of fear and death. Yet it didn't frighten her. She knew that he was on her side — more than Dr. Goodrich, or the nurses — he looked at her evenly, without embarrassment, and his face seemed to be saying: I know fear and I respect its power, but I am not afraid.

She looked into his eyes and quite suddenly he began to recede, to get smaller and smaller until he was no bigger than a doll. She remembered this happening to her as a child, when she was looking at something she especially loved or feared. The experience had always filled her with terror. (*"I am awake, I am truly awake, it can't be happening, I haven't moved, nothing has changed." "It was only a dream, dear." "I am really awake." "Only a dream."*)

Sands. Ugly little old doll. How wonderfully he was made. Almost human, the way he moved.

"I am not feeling very well," she said in a strong clear voice.

"Did you hear me, Mrs. Morrow?"

"Oh, yes . . . Oh, yes."

"We've found the parcel you threw into the lake."

"Oh, yes."

"Did you throw it away, or did Greeley?"

He came back, life-size.

"Greeley?" Lucille said.

"He may not have used that name. Will you look at this, please, Mrs. Morrow? Is this the man?"

He held out a picture and she looked at it, blinking slowly, trying to control the expression of her face. Her mind seemed to be working with extraordinary clarity. (I could pretend not to recognize the picture. But perhaps they can prove I knew him. I'll admit I know him, but nothing else, nothing else . . .)

"This is Greeley," Sands said. "He was the man who waited for you across the street from the hairdressing shop. He is dead."

"Dead?"

She had a sudden wild surge of hope. If this man was dead she had a chance. She would get out of here, she would *fight*.

"He was murdered," Sands said.

The hope drained out of her body like

blood from a wound. Her hands were icy, and her face had a stupid dazed expression.

"I am not trying to harry you, Mrs. Morrow, but to protect you. Someone has taken the trouble to kill Greeley on your account. Greeley was in the way — of something. Greeley was between you — and someone." His voice pressed, relentless, on her ears. "Who wants you dead?"

To frighten her, Sands thought, enough, but not too much . . .

"If I knew," Lucille said. "If I knew . . ."

"You know why."

"No."

"You gave Greeley fifty dollars?"

("Here, take this, it's all I've got." The little man grinning as if the bitter wind had swept up the corners of his mouth. "I figured on more, I figure it's worth it." "I'll get it for you." The wind piercing her thin coat. "Now wait a minute, I ain't been standing around here for my health. I know what was in that box. I looked." "Who gave it to you? Who told you to bring it to me?" "Offhand like this I can't remember." The grin again, though he looked cold and sick and ready to drop in his tracks. "I'll get more for you.")

"No," she said.

"One of your maids has already identified Greeley as the man who brought the box to your house. If I am to help you, Mrs. Morrow, I must know what was behind this thing. It is too crude and grotesque for a joke. And too dangerous to lie about."

She shivered. She could still feel the wind. It seemed to be blowing at her back, pushing her along toward the water, into the water. She felt an icy wave roll against her leg, and her forehead was bathed in sweat. Her head lolled and her mouth opened, sucking in the rush of water.

There was a movement in the room, a hand touching her lightly on the shoulder, Dr. Goodrich's voice saying, "That will be all, I think, for today," and Miss Parsons wiping off her forehead with a cloth.

At the door Lucille turned around. Sands was still watching her.

"Good-bye," she said clearly.

She gave him an intelligent, almost apologetic glance, as if she felt even yet the strange alliance between them. You and I — we both have secrets — there isn't time to tell them.

"Good-bye," Sands said.

She moved, heavily, out into the corridor. Beside her Miss Parsons chattered, trying to imitate Miss Scott and doing it badly.

Up the incline, past an old man bundled in a wheelchair who peered at her suspiciously over his blankets. A door. A girl sweeping the corridor, moving the broom in perfect unfaltering rhythm over the same spot of floor.

"Come, Doris," Miss Parsons said. "Let's do *this* corner now."

But Miss Parsons lacked Miss Scott's assurance. The girl Doris didn't look up or pause a second in her sweeping.

Miss Parsons hesitated and walked on. I'll go crazy if I have to stay here, she thought, I'll go *crazy*.

She locked the last door behind her and led Lucille into her room. Breathing hard, she came out again and handed the big key over to Miss Scott.

"Everything all right?" Miss Scott said.

"Fine."

"What's the matter with you? You look done in."

"Jitters," Miss Parsons said "Creeps. Whatever you want to call them."

"Cheer up. We all get them."

"When I think how many nurses actually end up here . . ."

"Well, for that matter," Miss Scott said practically, "look at how many of everything end up here, doctors, teachers, lawyers . . ."

"But more nurses."

"Oh, nuts," said Miss Scott. "Count your

blessings. This is the nicest ward in the hospital to work in. Should be, at the prices they pay and with me in charge."

"Even so."

"Oh, cheer up, Parsons." She smiled kindly, and instantly became businesslike again. "I'll get the word down to O.T. Mrs. Hammond stays up here. Dr. Nathan says she may have to be put in the continuous bath. Next week they're going to try metrazol on her."

Miss Parsons bit her lip. "Gosh, I hope — I hope I don't have to assist. Last year I saw a woman break both her legs in a treatment — the noise . . ."

"That's all changed now," Miss Scott said. "They use a curare injection to relax the muscles. It's quite marv— " She turned her head suddenly. Her alert ears had picked up a sound from Mrs. Morrow's room, like a retch or a low grunt.

Pushing Miss Parsons out of her way she ran noiselessly down the corridor. Mrs. Morrow might be sick again, as she was yesterday . . .

But Lucille was not sick. She was standing just inside the door, saying over and over again in a blank voice, "Cora? Cora? Cora?"

Cora Green was lying on the floor. She

had fallen forward on her face with her hands outstretched, and spilled around her were blue grapes like broken beads.

"Why, Cora," said Miss Scott.

She knelt down.

Why, Cora, you're dead.

CHAPTER 9

Quietly and quickly Miss Scott walked back to Lucille, thrust her out into the hall and locked the door.

"Come along, Mrs. Morrow. Let's find another room, shall we?"

(A door opened in Lucille's mind, and out popped Cora, giggling, "Really! Isn't she absurd?")

"Cora's not feeling well." There was a lilt in Miss Scott's voice, but the pressure of her fingers was businesslike. "She's had these attacks before. They always pass off."

(*Absurd, absurd,* screamed the little Cora, hilariously. *Really, oh, really, really.*)

"Oh, Miss Parsons, would you mind calling Dr. Laverne! Miss Green is ill."

In fact, said Miss Scott's wriggling eyebrow, Miss Green is deader than a doornail but let's keep it from the children.

"Oh," said Miss Parsons, paling. "Of course. Right away."

She fumbled for the telephone.

"Now, let me see, Mrs. Morrow," Miss Scott said. "It's just about time for O.T., isn't it? Are we all ready to go down?"

(The little Cora doubled up with mirth, her hands at her throat, choking with laughter. Choking . . . "Cora! Cora, you're poisoned — Cora." Cora went right on choking.)

"She was poisoned. In the grapes. They killed her," Lucille said. The words were clear cut in her brain, but they had lost their outlines in traveling to her tongue, and came out as a muffled jumble of syllables.

Miss Scott bent her head attentively, and looked as if she quite understood everything.

"You didn't hear me," Lucille said.

"Pardon?"

"You didn't hear me. She was killed. The grapes were for me."

"Now, now, nobody's going to take your nice grapes away from you. Don't you worry your pretty head about the grapes."

Lucille drew in her breath. If she spoke very very slowly and tried to control her tongue they would understand her. "Cora — Cora — was . . ."

Miss Scott smiled blankly. "Why, of course, Cora will be all right."

Lucille turned her anguished eyes to Miss Parsons, pleading. Miss Parsons tried to smile at her, like Miss Scott. Her lips drew back from her teeth but her eyes were stirred with panic. You're crazy, why, you're crazy as a bedbug, I'm afraid of you.

Dr. Laverne came in the door. He walked softly on his rubber-soled shoes but he had a big booming voice.

Lucille saw him lock the door behind him. He was carrying his instrument bag in one hand and he didn't palm the key as the nurses did, but put it in his coat pocket. It was so large that one end of it stuck out at the top of the pocket.

Lucille couldn't take her eyes off it. The key that would unlock everything. Escape from the hounds, set up a new trail. They have holed you up here, but if you can get the key . . .

Carefully she looked away. She must be very canny, not let them suspect anything. She knew that Cora had been poisoned but no one would ever believe her. They thought she was insane because she couldn't say the right words.

They didn't realize how clever she was. One more look at the key, to make sure it was there. Then she would pretend to be sick, or to faint, that was better. And when the doctor bent over her she would take the key. Through the doors and down the slopes and past the iron gate.

Clever, clever, she thought, and fell back

against Miss Scott's arm, and heard the doctor padding softly toward her.

"Watch your key, doctor," Miss Scott said pleasantly.

She didn't actually faint then, but she felt too tired to get up. She sagged against Miss Scott's knees. They were talking about her, but she was too tired to listen. They were urging her to do something, to move her legs, go through a door, behave yourself, lie down, room of your own. We feel that, we know that, we want you to, we are convinced, we, angels of mercy stepping delicately around the blood, so tenderly bathing the dead unfeeling flesh.

Time for lunch, time for rest, time to take a walk, time for Dr. Nathan, time for Dr. Goodrich, time for dinner.

Music, therapy, color movies, church, a dance, bridge.

So much time and never any of it your own, so many people and such shadows they all were. Only sometimes did a scene or a person seem real to her — the Filsinger twins, pressed close together, dancing dreamily to a Viennese waltz, Mrs. Hammond carefully dealing out a bridge hand and as carefully strewing the cards on the floor, Dr. Goodrich talking.

"The report on the autopsy is perfectly

clear, Mrs. Morrow. Miss Green died of heart failure."

No, no, no.

"Do you understand me, Mrs. Morrow? Miss Green has had a heart condition for some time. Her death was not a surprise to us. The autopsy was performed by a police surgeon and there was not the faintest evidence of poison."

"The grapes."

"The grapes were all tested, Mrs. Morrow."

Liar.

"Miss Green, Cora's sister, is perfectly satisfied with the report. Cora was apparently eating some of the grapes and a bit of skin got caught in her throat. She became panicky. You must have come into the room just then, and perhaps the sudden entrance, and the blockage in her throat . . ."

"Filthy sonofabitch lying cur," Lucille said distinctly. "Filthy stinking whoremaster . . ."

He waited patiently until she had finished, a little surprised, as always, by the secret vocabulary of women.

"There was no trace of any poison," he repeated. "I arranged for Cora's sister to come and see you. She's in the waiting room now."

Miss Janet Green had been reluctant to come to Penwood. She had been there so often, always to see Cora, always with a little bit of hope in her heart that this time Cora would be better, would actually want to come home. But three days ago Cora had died, and her death had had the same enigmatic quality as her life. Everything was perfectly clear on the surface but there were strange undercurrents.

Janet Green had attended the inquest, a little puzzled, a little bovine.

Quite incredible that Cora should panic over a bit of grape-skin. Her heart was bad, of course, and there was no evidence of anything else, but still . . .

After the inquest Dr. Goodrich had come over and spoken to her and told her about a woman called Mrs. Morrow who thought Cora had been poisoned.

"What nonsense!" Janet said, dabbing at her eyes with a damp handkerchief. "Poor Cora, everyone loved her."

"It is, of course, pure imagination on Mrs. Morrow's part, but that doesn't make it any easier for her. I want you to come to Penwood and talk to her."

"I? There's nothing I can do."

"It's possible that you can convince her you're perfectly satisfied with the inquest.

Cora told her a great deal about you. I think she'll look upon you as being on her side. That is, you are Cora's sister and would be most interested in the fact of Cora's death."

"As indeed I am," Janet said dryly. "I'm not quite satisfied. Are you?"

"Perhaps not. The only person who knows the facts is Mrs. Morrow."

"I see. So I'm to see her for two reasons, to talk, and to listen?"

"I have no right to ask you to do this, of course."

"That's all right," Janet said brusquely. "I'll do what I can."

She was a good-hearted woman. She liked to help people, and since Cora was dead and in no need of anything, she would help Mrs. Morrow.

She went at it firmly, telling Lucille in a calm kind voice that she was Cora's sister, that Cora had died of heart failure, she herself had attended the inquest. She was used to the hospital and not at all nervous, but there was something in Lucille's expression that made her uncomfortable. Lucille's mouth was twisted as if she was tasting Janet's words and finding them bitter.

And those eyes, Janet thought. Really quite hopeless.

She went on, however, and out of pity

even invented a lie, though inventions of the sort were foreign to her nature and very difficult for her.

"Cora was always afraid of choking, even when she was a child."

"She was ten years older than you," Lucille said. Her tongue felt thick but the words were audible.

Janet flushed. "I can remember hearing her tell about it."

"You mustn't treat me as if I'm stupid. Cora wasn't stupid. She knew right away that she'd been poisoned."

"I'm certain you're wrong. No one would want to harm Cora."

"Not Cora. Me. They were meant for me. She ate some when I was out of the room. When I came back she was sitting on her bed eating them."

"Slower, please, Mrs. Morrow. I can't understand you."

"I ran to her and told her the grapes were poisoned and tried to get them away from her, but it was too late. She was dead, instead of me."

The picture became suddenly clear to Janet. Cora had been sitting on the bed, eating the grapes, when Mrs. Morrow came in. Cora had looked up, smiling impishly, apologetically, because they weren't her grapes, after all. . . . The smile fading as Mrs. Morrow lunged across the room to grab the grapes away from her . . . "They're poisoned!"

Cora had been frightened to death.

It was all clear. It even accounted for so many of the grapes being spilled around the room. It was one of the things that had worried her — why Cora should have plucked so many of the grapes off the stem, if she had just been sitting there eating them in the ordinary way. But it was perfectly clear now. Everything was settled.

She explained it all to Dr. Goodrich, who seemed relieved, and then set out for home.

Off and on throughout the following week she thought of Lucille Morrow. She was sorry that she had not been able to do more for her, but also a little resentful because if it hadn't been for Lucille, Cora might still be living.

On Friday morning, the day after Cora's funeral, Janet returned to the office. She was head buyer for the French Salon at Hampton's, a department store, and she had a good deal of work to do before she went to New York for the spring clothes preview. But she didn't get as much work done as she'd hoped to, for about eleven o'clock a policeman came to see her.

Her secretary brought her his card, and Janet turned it over in her hand, frowning. Detective Inspector Sands. Never heard of him. Probably something about parking or driving through a red light. Still, an inspector. Perhaps my car's been stolen.

"Send him in." She leaned back in the big chair, filling it comfortably. She looked quite calm. It wasn't the first time she'd been visited by a policeman. Cora's misdemeanors had made her acquainted with a number of them.

But surely, she thought, even Cora couldn't be raising hell in hell. One corner of her mouth turned up in a regretful little smile.

"Miss Green? I'm Inspector Sands."

"Oh, yes. Sit down, will you?"

"I've come about your sister's death."

"Well." Janet raised her thick black eyebrows. "I thought that was settled at the inquest."

"The physical end of it, yes. . . . There is no doubt at all that your sister's death was accidental. It's Mrs. Morrow's connection with your sister that I'd like to know more about."

He sat down, holding his hat in his hands. Janet looked at him maternally. He seemed very frail for a policeman. Probably they had to take just anybody on the force nowadays, with so many able-bodied men drafted. Probably he doesn't get proper meals and rest, and certainly somebody should *do* something about his clothes.

Sands recognized her expression. He had seen it before, and it always caused him trouble.

Tomorrow I enroll with Charles Atlas, he thought.

"Dr. Goodrich and I talked it over," Janet said. "It wasn't the poor woman's fault that she killed Cora. Dr. Goodrich said she was actually very fond of Cora, and in telling her the grapes were poisoned she was trying to save Cora's life."

"That's why I'm here. On Saturday Miss Green died. On Friday you'd been to visit her. Did she say anything about Mrs. Morrow to you then?"

"Oh, she said a few things, I guess. Cora was such a chatterbox sometimes I didn't pay much attention. She did say that she liked her new roommate and felt sorry for her."

"Tell me, how many years was your sister at Penwood?"

"Off and on, for nearly ten years. She really liked it there. She was quite sane, you know, and very interested in the psychology of the patients."

"And not at all nervous about being with them?"

"Not at all."

"Isn't it odd, then, that she should have actually believed Mrs. Morrow when Mrs. Morrow told her the grapes were poisoned? She was accustomed to the fancies and vagaries of the other patients. Why did she take Mrs. Morrow seriously?"

"I never thought of that," Janet said with a frown. "Of course you're right. Cora would have said, 'Oh, nonsense,' or something like that. Unless — well, unless the grapes were really poisoned?"

"They weren't."

"I'm very confused. I thought everything was settled, and now — well, now, I don't know what happened."

"What happened is clear enough. Your sister died of shock. And why? Because I think she *believed* Mrs. Morrow, she was convinced that Mrs. Morrow was not insane, that someone was really trying to kill her."

"You sound," Janet said, "you sound as if you believe that too."

"Oh, yes. I do, indeed."

Janet looked skeptical. "Some of the patients at Penwood can be very convincing, you know."

"Yes. But your sister isn't the first of Mrs. Morrow's associates to die. She's the third."

"The — third?"

"Miss Green's death is the third. I believe it was accidental. The other two were deliberate murders. They remain unsolved."

He waited while Janet registered first shock at the murders, and then indignation that they were still unsolved. In his mind's eye he could see the three who had died: Mildred Morrow, young and plump and pretty; Eddy Greeley, a diseased and useless derelict; Cora Green, a harmless little old woman.

Each so dissimilar from the others, all having only one thing in common — Lucille Morrow.

"Well, I don't know what I can do to help," Janet said. "I'm sorry I can't remember more of what Cora said about Mrs. Morrow."

Sands rose. "That's all right. It was a slim chance, anyway."

"Well, I really am sorry," Janet said, and rose, too, and offered him her hand. "Good-bye. If there's anything more I can do . . ."

"No, thanks. Good-bye."

They shook hands and he went out, into the subdued whispering atmosphere of the

French Salon. As he passed through the store the air became warmer, the people noisier, the counters garish with Christmas. Perfume, gloves, specialty aisles, slightly soiled and marked-down underwear, clerks in felt Dutch bonnets, "The Newest Rage," "Anything on this table 29¢," "Give her — Hose!"

Throngs of housewives and college girls, harassed males and bewildered children, prams and elbows and tired feet and suffocating air.

He paused beside a tie counter to get his breath. That's what you see with your eyes open, he thought. The tired feet and shoulder-sag, the faces lined by pain or by poverty, the endless hurry not to get to some place, but to get out of some place.

But you could stand back and almost close your eyes and see only the happy bustling throng, joyous with Christmas spirit, happy, happy people in a happy, happy world.

Happy. Silly word. Rhymes with sappy and pappy.

The clerk came up. "Is there anything I can do for you?"

"No, thanks," Sands said. "Everything's been done for me."

He fought his way to the door, aware that

he was being childish and neurotic, that his own failure condemned him to see at the moment only the failure of others.

He passed through the revolving door on to Yonge Street and drew the cold air into his lungs. He felt better almost immediately, and thought, tomorrow I enroll with Charles Atlas *and* William Saroyan.

The street crowd was more purposeful in its bustling than the store crowd. The stenographers, bank clerks, truss-builders, typesetters, lawyers and elevator operators were all in search of food. The elevator operators picked up a hamburger and a cup of coffee at a White Spot. The stenographers ate chicken à la king jammed knee to knee in a Honey Dew, and the lawyers, with less drive and perhaps a more careful use of the privilege of pushing, headed for the Savarin on Bay Street.

On the corner a newsboy about seventy was urging everyone to read all about it in the *Globe and Mail.* About two o'clock he would be equally vociferous about the *Star* and *Tely* and around midnight he would appear again, this time with the *Globe and Mail* for the following day.

Heraclitus' state of flux, Sands thought. Not a flowing river, but a merry-go-round, highly mechanized, with the occasional brass ring for a free ride.

He bought a paper, and with it folded under his arm he walked to the parking lot to get his car.

While he was waiting for the attendant he opened the newspaper and read the want ads. Later he would read the whole thing, but the want ads were the most fascinating part to him. He could, offhand, tell anyone how much it cost to have facial hair permanently removed, how many cocker spaniels were lost and mechanics were needed, the telephone number of a practical nurse and what you did, supposing you owned a horse and the horse died.

Bird's-eye view of a city.

The attendant returned. Folding the paper again, Sands tipped him and climbed into his car. He forgot about lunch and drove back to his office instead.

The first person he saw when he opened the door was Sergeant D'arcy.

"Good afternoon, sir," D'arcy said.

When he talked, his prim little mouth moved as little as possible.

"Oh," Sands said. "What do you want?"

"Well, sir, as a matter of fact I'm not happy in Inspector Bascombe's department."

"That's too damn bad."

D'arcy flushed. "Well, I mean it, really. Mr. Bascombe is a truly intelligent man, but he is uncouth. He doesn't understand me. He keeps picking on me."

"And?"

"I told the Commissioner that my qualifications, educational and otherwise, were of more specific use in your department." The Commissioner was D'arcy's uncle by marriage. "I told him I'd be much happier working with you because you don't pick on me."

"Then it's about time I started," Sands said.

D'arcy took it as a joke and began to giggle. When he giggled the air whistled through his adenoids and the general effect was so unlovely that Sands' contempt turned momentarily into pity.

"Why you want to be a policeman, I don't know," he said.

"I feel that my qualifications, educational and . . ."

"Stop quoting yourself. Why doesn't uncle set you up in an interior-decorating business or something? You'd look all right lugging around bolts of velvet."

"That's the kind of remark that Mr. Bascombe makes," D'arcy said stiffly. "My uncle wouldn't like it if he heard you say that."

"Your uncle isn't going to hear," Sands said pleasantly. "Because if I ever catch you sniveling and tale-telling while you're in this office . . ."

"Then I'm really in?" D'arcy said. "This is very good of you, sir. I'm just terribly pleased."

"Get to work," Sands said, and went into his private office and slammed the door.

He picked up the inter-office phone and called Bascombe.

"Bascombe? D'arcy's changing hands again."

"What a shame," Bascombe said with a spurt of laughter. "I'll certainly miss him when I go to the can. Had your lunch?"

"No."

"I'll stand you to a blueplate special."

"What's behind this?"

"Nothing. I had a letter from Ellen yesterday."

"Oh."

"She's still in Hull but she's sick of the electrician, she wants to come home."

"I see. Yeah. You buy me a lunch to pay for my advice which you won't take?"

"What the hell, I don't need advice," Bascombe said. "I wired her the money to come home."

"That's swell," Sands said. "That's dandy.

Pardon me if I'm not hungry."

"She swears that this time she's learned her lesson."

"She's working her way nicely through grade school. They say the work is tough, but no doubt she likes it."

"What the hell, what else could I do, but send her the money? She's my wife."

"That's a technicality," Sands said and quietly put down the phone.

Things were normal again. D'arcy was back, Ellen was back. Ellen had caught the brass ring. Some day someone would put it through her nose, but in the meantime she was seeing the world and a hell of a lot of different kinds of bedroom wallpaper.

The phone rang. It was Bascombe, sounding more uncertain now.

"All right," he said. "So what do you think I should do, smarty pants?"

"Lock the apartment and disappear. See a lawyer, make some arrangements to give her an allowance if your conscience bothers you. The essential fact is not that Ellen is a tramp, but that she wouldn't be one if she gave a damn about you or ever had. It's not a physical thing, she's not insatiable. She's just one of these low-grade morons who wants love as it is in the movies. Romance, soft lights and sweet music. All of the trimmings and none of the repercussions. Can be done, but not by Ellen. She's not bright enough."

There was a silence. Then Bascombe said, "The blueplate offer still holds."

"All right. I'll pick you up on my way down."

During lunch they didn't mention Ellen. They talked about the Morrow case. Bascombe's department had had nothing to do with it since Lucille Morrow had been found. But he had a professional interest in the case, and he listened intently to the story of Cora Green's death.

"Three of them," he said when Sands had finished. "Damn odd."

"Miss Green's death was, of course, an accident. It wasn't planned or even imagined by the person responsible for the other two. But the hellish part of it is, her death is serving a purpose. It's driving Mrs. Morrow past the borderline of sanity. And that, I believe, is the ultimate motive — to get Mrs. Morrow. The driving power behind it is hate. Mrs. Morrow must be made to suffer, perhaps eventually she must be killed. But the present setup may stand. Someone is getting an exquisite pleasure in seeing Mrs. Morrow trying to cling to the wreck of her mind."

"Jes—us," Bascombe said. "Damn funny the mere sight of an amputated finger would send her crazy, though."

"It didn't. It wasn't the finger itself, but her own state of mind at the time and the *implications* of the finger. A dead finger meant to her a dead woman — Mildred, the first wife; and a death warning to her, the second wife. Who can tell, if she doesn't? Perhaps to her it was a sexual symbol, a token of her marriage." He looked at Bascombe and added softly, "And perhaps it meant more, much more than that.

"Of course it's a member of her family. No one else could hate her so thoroughly, or know enough of her weaknesses to attempt such a refined sport as driving her insane. Greeley did his share in helping. To a woman who has lived a cultured, quiet, comfortable life the mere contact with a man like Greeley must have been a shock. And the sending of the finger was a piece of mental sadism that I've rarely seen equaled."

"Who in hell would even *think* of sending a finger? And where did it come from?"

"The Morrow family can offer no suggestions. They are united on one thing — that the police have no right to bother them, that they are having enough trouble as it is. I questioned them at their house. When I was leaving, Dr. Morrow took me aside and asked me everything about the finger. He looked frightened, as if he knew quite a lot that he wasn't telling."

"The Morrow women," Bascombe said dryly, "have bad luck."

"But the method is getting more genteel. From axes to suggestion. I've gone through all the police files and press clippings on Mildred Morrow. The first person to check in a wife-murder is, of course, the husband. Dr. Morrow not only had a complete alibi but the news of his wife's death put him in a hospital with brain fever. There's nothing phony there. The hospital records and charts stand, and the woman whose baby he was delivering at the time Mildred was killed is still living and remembers the night very well. All this, and the fact that he had no possible motive, puts Dr. Morrow in the clear."

"Morrow seems to have bad luck too." Bascombe finished a piece of pie and pushed the plate away. "Don't we all?"

"You picked yours."

"Don't labor the point. Coming?"

Sands said he was not going back to the office. He had an appointment at the Ford Hotel.

Fifteen minutes later he was facing Lieutenant Frome across a small writing desk at the Ford.

Frome was very stiff and very military. In clipped tones he told Sands that he had recently finished his Transport Officer's course at the Canadian Driving and Maintenance School at Woodworth. He was now waiting to be transferred overseas. It was his last furlough and he had intended to spend it getting married. How he actually was spending it was sitting around this dreary hotel waiting for Polly Morrow to make up her mind.

As he talked Frome became less a soldier and more an ordinary man with a grievance.

"I can't understand it," he told Sands. "She's got some idea in her head that I've walked out on her. What I did was come down here. The rest of the family didn't want me there. Why should they? I'm a stranger to them." He forgot that Sands was a policeman on official business. Sands let him talk uninterrupted. He liked listening to people's problems, it was a little more personal than the want ads.

"Martin's been O.K.," Frome said. "He says Polly likes to boss people around until there's an emergency and then she has to be bossed. I don't understand women. I'm from the West, Alberta. Women don't act like this out there."

"Don't they," Sands murmured.

"In fact, the whole thing has been a mess from the time I met her family. Practically before we said hello we had to run into a train wreck."

"Oh? Who was with you?"

"Polly and her father and Martin. I was so damn nervous anyway about meeting her family — I'd only known *her* for three weeks. And then running into that mess and ending up by picking up bodies . . ." He looked bitterly at Sands, as if Sands had engineered the whole thing. "All right. What did you want to ask me?"

Sands smiled. "Nothing. Not a thing. Just dropped in to see how you were."

Still smiling, he walked across the lobby, pausing at the door to wave his hand cheerfully.

"Everybody's crazy," Lieutenant Frome told the bartender some time later. "Everyone's crazy but me."

"Sure," the bartender said. "Sure."

CHAPTER 10

On the day of Cora's death, Lucille was transferred to a room of her own and put in the charge of a special nurse.

Miss Eustace had a highly specialized and difficult job. She called herself a free-lance psychiatric nurse. She worked in institutions and private homes, taking over twenty-four-hour-a-day care of violent or depressed patients to prevent them from doing harm to themselves or to others.

Her reputation and her wages were high, and she was regarded with awe by the other nurses, who felt the strain of even eight-hour duty on a disturbed ward. Over forty now, Miss Eustace considered herself a dull woman and was always surprised when she was praised for her skill and endurance and patience. In addition to these qualities Miss Eustace had a firm belief in God, a working knowledge of judo, and the ability to sleep and awaken as quickly as a dog. Only once had she been injured on a case, and that had been with one of her own knitting needles. She subsequently gave up knitting, and for amusement she played solitaire and wrote letters or simply talked.

Lucille refused food for nearly a week and on the fourth day Miss Eustace force-fed her by tube.

When it was over Miss Eustace said calmly, "It's very undignified, isn't it? Especially for a pretty woman like you."

Almost unconsciously Lucille turned her head toward the mesh-covered mirror. Pretty? Me? Where is my hair?

"Tonight we'll have a bit of soup together," Miss Eustace continued. "You can't possibly starve yourself to death, you know. It takes too long."

Miss Scott, trained in a different tradition, would have been horrified to hear Miss Eustace speaking of "death" or "starving" to a patient. On the level of pure theory Miss Scott may have been right, but Miss Eustace got results. For supper Lucille had a bowl of soup and a custard and some faint trace of color returned to her pallid drawn face.

But she was losing weight rapidly. Her clothes sagged on her body, and there were hollows beneath her cheekbones and a little sac of flesh under her chin. She never bothered to comb her hair and had to be told when to wash her hands. Though she seemed to listen quite attentively when Miss

Eustace was talking, she rarely answered, and what talking she did was at night after she had been given a sedative. At these times she was like a person who, after a certain number of drinks, feels he is thinking and talking very clearly and brilliantly, with no consciousness of his blurred speech.

Miss Eustace went on playing solitaire and marking down her score. Out of one hundred and forty-nine games she had only won eleven. (But then it was, she wrote to her mother, a very difficult type of solitaire.)

"All of it is Mildred's fault," Lucille muttered into the shadows. "Mildred . . ."

("My case is just popping off to sleep," Miss Eustace wrote, steadily. "So please excuse the writing as just the floor light is on and it isn't very bright in here.")

"Miss Eustace!"

"Here I am," Miss Eustace said pleasantly. "Would you like a drink?"

"I keep thinking about Mildred."

"Turn over and think about something else."

"What have they done with my hair?"

("She wants to know what they've done with her hair," Miss Eustace wrote. "They do think of quite the oddest things to say sometimes.")

Lucille turned over in the bed. Think

about something else. Not about Mildred. But look, see Mildred's hair. How coarse it looked, each hair as thick as a tube, moving, writhing like snakes, oh, Miss Eustace, oh, please God.

("I really feel sorriest of all for the family. After all, they're still sane. My case's family came today, visitors' day, but they couldn't see her, Dr. Goodrich's orders.")

The snakes writhed and bled in spurts, covering Mildred's face with their blood — go away, go away — I won't look at you. . . .

"Bloody, bloody," she said, softly.

("The language some of them use! I declare, for a Christian woman, I do know some of the awfullest words. I'd blush to repeat them. It even disturbs me when someone refers to our darling Lassie as a 'bitch.' I just can't get used to it. Give Lassie a bone for me and tell her I'll be coming home soon.")

"I can't sleep," Lucille said.

"You're trying too hard. Just close your eyes and think of something nice and soothing, like rain or grass waving or trees."

Grass. I am thinking of grass and trees. The park, late at night, black, but moving, astir with shapes and shadows — be careful, look over your shoulder, there is something there — careful! Ah. It's only Martin, don't be afraid. Martin? Is it Martin, or Edith? It's too dark, I don't know. But it's a friend, I can tell. Such a nice face, so wide and frank and candid.

Suddenly it closed up like a fist. Where the eyes and mouth had been there were only folds of skin, and two holes for a nose and little buds of ears.

"I can't stand it! I can't stand it!"

"What can't you stand? You just tell me and we'll fix it in a jiffy."

"I see — things . . ."

"How about some nice warm milk? I find warm milk puts me off just like that."

"No — no . . ."

The warm milk was sent for, but when it arrived Lucille couldn't drink it.

"It smells bad."

"Why, it smells perfectly all right to me. Look, I'll take a sip first, how would that be?"

"It's bad."

Miss Eustace took a number of sips to encourage her and pretty soon the milk was gone. Refreshed, Miss Eustace returned to her letter.

The smell of the milk lingered in the room, very faint and subtle, like the smell of blood or fresh snow.

"The poor woman really thinks someone

is trying to poison her." Miss Eustace's pen moved in slow rhythm across the page. "I have found the best thing to do is to take a taste of everything before she does. It reassures her. Perhaps it's not very sanitary, *but!*")

The scratching of the pen was barely audible but Lucille's ears magnified the sound. The sedative was wearing off, leaving her nerves raw and her senses too acute. Though she hadn't drunk the milk, the taste lingered on her tongue, a furry gray-white sickness. The giant claws of the pen dug deep into the paper, and Miss Eustace's quiet breathing was loud as a wind.

She turned over again. The blankets were heavy on top of her, painful and suffocating. She flung them off, and cool air struck her bare legs, and she began to shiver.

Silently Miss Eustace crossed the room and lowered the window.

"Do you want me to rub your back?"

"No."

"It might help. Can't have any more sedatives tonight, you know."

In a sudden fury Lucille told her what she could do with all sedatives.

Miss Eustace remained calm. "Now, now."

"You drank all my milk. *I* wanted it!"

"We'll get you some more."

"I wanted *that* milk."

Miss Eustace walked briskly into the bathroom and came back with a box of talcum powder.

"Roll over. We'll try a back rub."

"No!" Like a child she kept saying "No!" even while she was complying.

Miss Eustace turned back her sleeves, revealing the highly developed forearm muscles that mark an experienced nurse.

Up and down. Across and around. As she worked Miss Eustace talked in a monotone about her mother, her dog Lassie, her pretty sister who had just been married.

At first the pain of her hands was unbearable to Lucille, but gradually she relaxed, and flung herself on the mercy of her dreams.

Miss Eustace opened the window and sat down on the edge of her cot to take off her slippers. The last thing she did before she went to bed was to cover Lucille.

Lucille tossed and turned in her sleep under the light blankets that seemed to bind her legs and waist. Her sleeping mind was alive and sentient in her fingers, her nipples, her hips, her thighs, the sensitive palms of her feet; but it seemed to lie caught in a net of words. *Miss Eustace my father and my murther flusttering in the aviary tower in vanity all inanity ah night my sweethurt take me out of the dunjuan through the griefclanging door to the godpeace of sir night.* She struggled in the web of words, the blankets fell to the floor, and the web parted.

Her dreaming mind moved in images across the unforgotten fields of the unconscious, seen forever for the first time. Across the footstippled snow she moved like a gull, like a ghoul, leaving no track, casting no shadow. The iron gate stood ajar behind her, the sky curved over her head, poised and ponderous like an unclosed trap. Along the highway which ran like a ruler to the house where she must go, a line of cars went by, their wheels mourning on the road. Their drivers were faceless with grief and doubt and malice: Polly, Martin, Andrew, Edith, faceless things passing to nothingness on the straight and narrow assembly-line of doom.

A man in gray clothes whose facelessness looked four ways stopped his car by the gate, and the line of cars extending to the horizon stopped. He stretched out a gray aspen-quaking hand to assist her and the door of the car closed behind her softly like a mouth. The gray car moved on the gray road and the line of cars began to hurry hurry. The driver scanned the road ahead, and the woman in the back seat, and the bloody snow in the ditch, with omniscient eyelessness.

The car dissolved around her like a mist and the funereal procession went on forever over other hills, white rising hills pimpled with blood. She was alone among the pines, walking in a tunnel of dark-dripping pines which led to the house. She could see its white portico like a grinning mouth with long teeth, grinning in pain or menace. Behind the smiling pillars the doors and windows blazed with light, but she knew there was nobody home.

As she approached, the lights faded slowly like recognition in dying eyes, and the portico grinned alone like a jawbone bared by worms. Passing a pillar she touched it with her hand and felt the rotting plaster. Within the house a faint stench of mold hung in the air like a souring regret. Moving in the earthy darkness she knew it was a tomb she had entered. It was terrible to step into a tomb, but she must find what she had come to get. The book of life which was the book of death.

Suddenly the house was as friendly and

multiform as a large family spawned suddenly like mushrooms. As she climbed the hunched stairs the walls nudged her with obscene expectancy, the treads creaked like the malicious cackle of children, the curtains on the landing curved outward and divided like fingers to pinch her buttocks and stroke her thighs. She took a knife from her bosom and cut them away, and the severed fingers fell down and danced like babies at her feet.

I must find the book, her fear said, and she went to her room and opened the bureau drawer. The Sangraal radiance of the book lit the room, and she saw it as she remembered it and knew she was remembering it, knew she was dreaming. *Thank God,* she said or dreamed, with the diary in her hands. *Thank God, no one has taken it.* She opened the book, the cover came off like the lid of a box, and the finger wriggled and squirmed inside like a mangled worm.

Out of the grinning tomb the gravestench house she ran with her hair coiling on her head like snakes like long dead nervous hands. The gray car came up to the door and the gray man led her into the little room behind the gathered curtains, where the dead slept on rollers under gravestench flowers. The long gray-curtained car moved away on rollers through the maze of streets cast over the city like a concrete net, along the gelid lake, the hill-flanked forests, beyond the triune towers, the many-nippled mountains into space which expanded utterly as they moved into bright anguished light beyond through the hard and alien blaze to the extreme edge. The bleak and brilliant sword-edge of death.

The lights at Penwood are never out. At night they are dimmed to give the illusion that darkness and sleep come naturally here as they do in the other world, but even at midnight and from a distance you can see the glow of Penwood.

There were always night noises. Someone screamed, someone wanted to go to the bathroom; or someone died and the stretcher rolled softly up and down the inclines.

In the morning the roosters crowed, the cows made their sad sounds, the night nurses washed their patients and went off duty, and another day began. Breakfast, doctors' rounds, occupational therapy, lunch, rest, walk outside or in gym, private talks in doctors' offices, dinner, music and card games, bed.

The routine was subject to sudden changes. Wet packs or continual baths had to be given, or Miss Sims might obey her hidden voice and defile herself with food at the table, or Miss Filsinger might get out of the dining room with a forbidden spoon.

Miss Eustace woke early, and was immediately alert. Lucille was stirring but she hadn't opened her eyes, so Miss Eustace used the bathroom first. She washed her face and hands, cleaned her teeth thoroughly, and put on a fresh uniform.

Returning, she found Lucille awake.

"Good morning. Have a nice sleep?"

"Is it morning?" Lucille said.

"Oh my, yes. But it doesn't seem like it, does it? That's the one thing I don't like about winter, getting up before the sun."

While she talked she glanced with a professional eye at Lucille. She seemed rested and quite calm. Though Miss Eustace knew the calmness wouldn't last, she always considered it a good idea to take advantage of even a momentary improvement.

"Let's go down to breakfast this morning," she said cheerfully. "Some new faces would be good for you. Certainly you must be pretty tired of mine."

Lucille looked a little surprised. She hadn't, until this moment, been conscious that Miss Eustace had a face. Miss Eustace was uniform and authority, a starched white impersonalized symbol of "we."

"Let's wear the red dress. There's something so cheery about red on a winter morning, I find."

Lucille had no answer to this. None was possible. Miss Eustace had made up her mind that she, Lucille, in a red dress on a winter morning, should go down to breakfast.

"It's like a nursery school," she said.

"What is?"

"This place."

Miss Eustace laughed. "I suppose it is. Here's your toothbrush."

While Lucille was dressing, Miss Eustace made the two beds, timing herself by her watch. Two minutes for Lucille's bed, one minute, thirty-seven seconds for her own. With pride she marked the times down on her solitaire score pad.

Before she left she opened two windows wide to give the room a good airing, hung up Lucille's nightgown in the closet, and put her own wrinkled uniform in a laundry bag. Then, with a clear conscience and a good appetite, she went down to breakfast.

The dining room was quiet and orderly. The patients ate at small round tables in groups of three or four.

Automatically Lucille walked to the table

where she had sat before with Cora and the Filsinger twins.

Miss Eustace said "Good morning," to the twins, and then seated Lucille and herself.

"We personally don't want you here," Mary Filsinger said. "We like a table to ourselves. I've told the superintendent so a dozen times, haven't I, Betty?"

"I don't know," Betty said, with her mouth full.

"Don't stuff your mouth so. It's disgusting. Chew one hundred times."

"I can swallow everything whole," Betty explained proudly to Miss Eustace.

"Don't talk to her," Mary said. "She's a spy."

Smiling and calm Miss Eustace began to talk about her house in the country and what she had for breakfast there and how her tulip tree first blossomed in the spring and when the blossoms fell off the leaves appeared.

"What color blossoms?" Mary asked, suspiciously.

"Pale pink, almost white, really."

"That's very funny about the leaves. I don't believe it for a minute."

"It's true," Lucille said suddenly. "I had a tulip tree, too."

"I wish I had one," Betty said.

Her sister touched her hand. "I'll buy you one."

"You always say that and you never do."

"Ungrateful liar."

"I'll swallow something whole if you call me that."

"Oh, Betty, don't! Darling, please don't!"

A maid arrived with orange juice, oatmeal cooked with raisins and a covered dish of eggs on toast.

Lover-like, the twins quarreled, while Miss Eustace talked about dogs. Collies were nice, and so were cocker spaniels, but she preferred Airedales, really. They were very faithful.

"Cats are best," said Mary, unable to resist Miss Eustace's dangling bait. "We like cats best of all."

"Well, cats are nice too," Miss Eustace agreed. "What do you like best, Mrs. Morrow?"

"Oh, I don't know," Lucille said. "Dogs, I guess."

"Dogs are vicious," Mary said, and closed her mouth decisively on a piece of toast.

"Some of them are, of course," Miss Eustace went on. "It depends mostly on the training and to a certain extent on heredity.

I personally have never been able to quite trust a chow, for instance."

"I'd rather have a tulip tree," Betty said.

Mary leaned over and muttered something in her ear but Betty tossed her head and looked scornful.

Miss Eustace watched Lucille out of the corner of her eye to see if the scene interested her or upset her. She noted with approval that Lucille had eaten half of her oatmeal, and, though she didn't talk voluntarily herself, except for the remark about her tulip tree, she seemed to be following the conversation.

We should have quite a good day, Miss Eustace thought, and felt pleased with herself.

The twins were fighting again, in low voices but with a great many flashing glances and passionate gestures. Finally Mary retreated into cold silence, and it was then that Miss Eustace saw her pick up her spoon and tuck it carefully into the bun of hair at the back of her head.

With a furtive glance around the room Mary rose and made for the door. Miss Eustace rose too.

"We're not supposed to take spoons out of the dining-room," she said kindly. "Put it back please."

"Spoon?" Mary cried in great surprise. "What spoon?"

"Put it back."

"I don't know what you're talking about."

The nurse in charge of the dining room was making her way toward them between the tables. She had the spoon out of Mary's hair before Mary was aware it was missing.

"Now, Mary," she said. "You know better than to do that. This is the second time this week."

"I'm running away," Mary cried. "I'm leaving her flat. She can't treat me like that and get away with it! I'm running away so she'll know what it's like to be left with no one to look after her!"

"I'll swallow something," Betty said calmly, and before anyone could stop her she had removed her ring from her finger and popped it in her mouth. Gulping and gasping she was dragged out of the room and pounded vigorously on the back by the nurse. But it was too late, the ring had already joined the collection of other articles in Betty's stomach.

The twins departed in disgrace with Miss Scott.

"Her insides must be a regular museum," the dining-room nurse said to Miss Eustace. "I'm going to catch it for this."

"It wasn't your fault at all," Miss Eustace said and returned to the table to finish her breakfast.

The episode had apparently made no impression on Lucille. She was intent on her toast, breaking it up into small pieces and arranging them symmetrically around the plate.

She's being very co-operative, Miss Eustace thought, she's really trying to eat.

Aloud she said, "Sugar for your coffee?"

"Yes, thanks."

The fat pink sugar bowl was passed. Lucille would not touch it, its flesh was too pink, too perfect. Not real flesh at all, she thought, but she knew it was because she could see it breathing.

Miss Eustace's spoon clanged against the grains of sugar. "One or two?"

"One."

"There. Stir it up before you drink it. No, dear, stir it up first."

She picked up her spoon, dreading the feel of it. Everything was alive, everything hurt. She was hurting the spoon, and though it looked stupid and inert it was hurting her in return, digging into her fingers.

"Not so *hard*, Mrs. Morrow."

Round the cup the spoon dashed in fury

and pain, stirring up the hot muddy waves and all the little alive things. She swallowed them, in triumph because she had won, and in despair, because, swallowed and out of sight, they would take vengeance on her.

Everything was alive. The floor that hurt your shoes that hurt your feet. The napkin that touched your dress that pressed against your thighs. Pain everywhere.

No privacy. You could never be alone. You always had to touch things and have them touch you. You had to swallow and be swallowed, have things inside you — alive things . . .

Her shoulders began to twitch.

She's impatient to leave, Miss Eustace thought. A good sign. Usually she just wants to stay where I've put her.

Miss Eustace rose. Callously her feet struck the floor, roughly she folded the napkins.

"Come along and we'll get the mail."

She put out her hand as if to help Lucille up. Lucille stared at the hand, and a shriek began to rise up inside her, making her throat raw and thick.

Miss Eustace saw the screaming eyes and began to talk fast and at the same time to coax her with gentle fingers out into the corridor.

The mail — push — what did she suppose she'd get this morning? — push — you never could tell with mail — parcels were the best, though . . .

Arm in arm, close, intimate, they strolled down the corridor.

They stopped at the mail desk. Andrew's daily box of flowers had arrived, but the incoming mail had not come yet and the girl behind the wicket was looking over the patients' outgoing mail. She picked up an envelope labeled in red crayon, "Wother."

"Look at this," she said, and passed the letter through the wicket to Miss Eustace. "He writes dozens of them every day."

"Wother? What's that?"

"He inverts his M's. He means his mother. I can't let his letters go out, I have to take them in to Dr. Nathan. They upset his mother terribly because all the boy does is complain."

"Hush," said Miss Eustace with a frown toward Lucille.

But Lucille hadn't heard anything. She was standing with her arms tight around the box of flowers. Brutally, the box hugged her breasts, and she embraced the pain.

"Though I just hate to suppress any letters," the girl said. "It's against my principles."

"Dear Wother," Miss Eustace read. "I can't stand it any longer the inflationary bargains of the state of the world, wother they are cruel to we they hate we and hardly any consequence could eventuate under the status quo of"

It was not signed but there was a row of X's at the bottom.

"Such a pity," said Miss Eustace, sighing. "I always say, it's the family that suffers most." She raised her voice. "Mrs. Morrow, you're crushing the box. Shall we go back up now or do you want to wait for the mail?"

"I don't know," Lucille said.

"Then I suppose we might as well wait. Shall we open the flowers?"

Lucille's grasp on the box tightened for an instant and then quite suddenly her fingers relaxed and the box fell on the floor. The lid came off and there was a spill of violets.

"Oh, the darlings," said Miss Eustace, picking them up. "Aren't they grand? Such an earthy smell, somehow." She nuzzled them while Lucille watched, suffering in silence for the violets, the long-limbed delicate children, too delicate to breathe and so, dead, and blue in the face, giving off the smell of earth, earth-buried coffins.

The live floor quivered under her feet, the air touched her cheeks and arms, its caress a warning and a threat, and the violets returned to life. They had only been holding their breath like Cora, and their little bruised faces puckered in pain! *Oh, I hurt, I hurt, and what have I done? Oh, what have I done?*

So tight and sad did the little faces become that they turned into eyes, damp blue eyes dragging their limp and single legs behind them into the box.

"Here you are," Miss Eustace said, passing the box to her. "Why, they're just the color of your eyes."

Lucille felt the sharp corner of the box touch her arm. The pain was so intense and unbearable that she had to reach out and grab the box and thrust the corner of it into her breast like a knife.

I have died. I am dead.

She smiled, and clutching the symbol of death, she moved silently and swiftly down the corridor.

"Mrs. Morrow, wait for me!" Miss Eustace caught up with her, panting. "Well, I declare, I didn't know you were in that much of a hurry. Were you going somewhere?"

"Out."

"Out where?"

"I want some fresh air."

"Oh, you do?" Miss Eustace said, half-pleased, half-suspicious.

"I want some fresh air."

"Well, let's wait a bit until the sun gets stronger, then we'll go out on the roof garden, there's such a pretty view from there. Wait here a minute and I'll go back for the mail."

Miss Eustace returned to the wicket, moving in a kind of sideways fashion so that she could keep Lucille in sight. Lucille made no attempt to get away from her. She stood, straight and alert, as if she was standing guard over something precious to her.

Miss Eustace came back. "Here's a letter for you, dear. Now aren't you glad we waited?"

Lucille wouldn't take the letter so Miss Eustace put it in the pocket of her uniform. So *unnatural* not to be interested in mail, she thought, and tried again when they reached the room.

"Here's your letter. You can read it while I'm doing the chart. Sit down right there. I'll put the flowers in water."

She settled Lucille in a chair and placed the letter on her lap. Then, humming softly, she went into the bathroom and filled a Monel vase with water. She was always excited by mail, other people's as well as her own. Even the most commonplace observations on the weather were glamorous when sealed and postmarked, with privacy protected by His Majesty, King George VI.

I wonder who it's from, she thought, and returned to the room. "Do you want me to read it to you?"

"I don't care."

Miss Eustace, thrilled, slit the envelope with an efficient thumbnail.

"It's signed 'Edith.' I always peek at the end of a letter just to see who it's from. Well, here goes. 'Dear Lucille: I hope you received the chocolates and pillow rest I sent day before yesterday.' Well, of course, we did, didn't we? Those back rests are very comfy. 'It is very difficult to get chocolates these days, one has to stand in line.' Wasn't it silly of you to destroy them when she went to so much trouble to buy them?"

Lucille turned her head and looked deliberately out of the window. *It is very difficult to get poisoned chocolates these days, one has to stand in line.*

" 'We all miss you a great deal, though I feel so hopeless saying it because I know you won't believe it.' "

I feel so hopeless.

" 'Everything is such a mess. The policeman Sands was here again, talking about the train wreck. You remember that afternoon? I don't know what he was getting at, but whoever did anything to you, Lucille, it wasn't me, Lucille, it was not me! I don't know, I can't figure anything out any more. I have this sick headache nearly all the time and Martin is driving me crazy.' "

"She isn't very cheerful, is she?" said Miss Eustace in disapproval. "Shall I go on?"

"Go on."

"Very well. 'They have always seemed like my own children to me, the two of them, and now, I don't know, I look at them and they're like strangers. Meals are the worst time. We watch each other. That doesn't sound like much, but it's terrible — we watch each other.' "

Silly woman, thought Miss Eustace, and turned the page.

" 'I know Andrew wouldn't like me to be writing a letter like this. But, Lucille, you're the only one I can talk to now. I feel I'd rather be there with you, I've always liked and trusted you.' "

I've always loathed and been jealous of you. We watched each other.

" 'Everything is so mixed up. Do you remember the night Giles came and I said, God help me, that we were a happy family? I feel this is a judgment on me for my smugness and wickedness. I don't know how it will all end.' "

This is a judgment on me for my wickedness. It will all end.

"That's all," said Miss Eustace.

That is all. It will all end and that is all.

Miss Eustace returned the letter to its envelope, her movements brisk because she was annoyed. People shouldn't write problem letters. Letters should be nice and homey and rather dull.

"Let's bundle all up and get some nice fresh air, shall we?"

Lucille didn't move. She sat, heavy and inert, while Miss Eustace lifted her arms into her coat and tied a scarf around her head and put on her gloves.

The roof garden glittered in the sun. Snow clung to the high fence, and where the strands of barbed wire ran around the top, there were globules of snow caught on the barbs.

Slowly Lucille walked over to the fence and put her hand on it. Snow sifted down on her upturned face, touching her eyelids lightly and coldly. She looked down through the fence and saw little people walking, their tracks behind them in the snow the only sign that they were real. So tiny and futile they seemed from a distance, like the skiers in the park.

Futile, futile, she thought and pressed her forehead hard against the fence, branding her flesh with a diamond.

"Goodness, I just can't look down from high places," Miss Eustace said. "It makes me quite dizzy."

She looked down anyway, shivering with cold and dread delight. Then she stepped back, and squinted her eyes against the sun. She breathed deeply because she didn't get much fresh air in her job and she had to get as much of it as she could when the chance came.

In — hold — out — hold — in — hold . . .

Miss Eustace felt glad to be alive.

Lucille remained pressed against the fence. She did not feel the cold, the pain, the heat of the sun. She was not aware of Miss Eustace behind her. She looked down, her eyes strained. The snow burst into orange flame, the sharp black shadows pointed at her, the smoke curled up at her, the windows stared at her, the wind went past whispering, it will all end.

In and out Miss Eustace breathed. She was beginning to wheeze a little but when she spoke she sounded triumphant.

"One hundred. Phew! I didn't realize just

breathing was such hard work. Still, I always say there's practically nothing the matter with anybody that one hundred deep breaths won't cure. Shall we walk a bit now?"

Lucille didn't answer, but Miss Eustace was feeling too invigorated to care. She strode away, planting her feet firmly, making nice clear tracks in the snow.

Twenty strides north, twenty strides south, in the rising wind.

It will all end.

"If you don't move around a bit, Mrs. Morrow, you'll be cold."

I will be burned in the snow they are waiting for me it will all end.

"No, really, you mustn't take your gloves off, dear, your hands will freeze."

She could feel Miss Eustace coming up behind her, but she didn't hurry with the second glove, she didn't even look to see what she was doing. She was filled with a great power because for the first time in weeks she knew now what she must do. Miss Eustace, no one, could stop her.

Her hands clung to the fence like eagle's claws, and she began to climb. Slowly. There was no hurry. She braced herself by catching the heels of her shoes in the fence holes, and up she climbed, bent double, her coat flapping around her.

Miss Eustace screamed "Stop!" and caught hold of one of her ankles and pulled. The heel of the other shoe came down viciously on the bridge of her nose and there was a crunch of bone and a spurt of blood. Miss Eustace lurched back screaming and wiping the blood out of her eyes.

"Come back! Come back!"

No — no — this is a judgment on me for my wickedness . . .

The barbed wire tore her hands and her face, but she felt nothing, made no sound. At the top she hoisted herself over, clumsily, but with great strength. Her coat caught on a barb and for a second she hung suspended in the air, a grotesque thing, bleeding and flapping.

Then the threads of the coat broke and she fell. Her big black shadow slid quietly down the wall of the building.

PART THREE

The Hounds

CHAPTER 11

"Mr. Sands?"

"Yes. Sit down, Miss Morrow."

"Mr. Sands, is this the end of it? It *must* be the end of it. She's dead now — the inquest is over — she's going to be buried this afternoon. . . ."

"Why not sit down?" Sands said and waited while Polly let herself drop into a chair.

She wore a black dress and a dark fur coat and the brim of her black hat shaded her eyes. She looked thinner than he remembered her, and more vulnerable. She kept her head down when she talked as if she was trying to hide behind her hat.

"I don't know why I came here. To get away from the family, I guess, and the smell of those damned flowers. Calla lilies. I feel as if they're sprouting out of my ears."

"They aren't."

She gave a tight little smile. "Nice to know. Anyway, I haven't any reason for being here, I haven't anything to tell you. I guess — well, I wanted someone to talk to."

"Normal."

"It is? Most people would say it's very abnormal to be dashing around town on the morning of your stepmother's funeral. Especially after the way she died. Dr. Goodrich said it's humanly impossible for anyone to scale that fence. Yet she did it." She bit her underlip. "Isn't that just like Lucille? A surprise to the very end. Not one of us really knew a damn thing about her because she didn't talk about herself. How *can* you know anything about a person without the evidence of her own words? And even then . . ."

"Yes, even then," Sands said.

"What a mess." She stared moodily at a corner of the desk. "What a filthy mess."

"You sound as if you're about to say, what have I done to deserve all this?"

"Well, I *do* say it. What have I?"

"I wouldn't know. But if you're looking for any system of logic in this world, in terms of human justice, you're younger than I thought."

"Twenty-five. But I've never been young."

"Women are notoriously fond of that cliché," Sands said. "Possibly there's some truth in it. Girls are usually held more responsible for their behavior than boys, and any sort of responsibility is aging."

Perhaps mine most of all, he thought. The collection of an eye for an eye. A mind for a mind.

She raised her head and looked at him. "You've changed quite a bit since I saw you years ago."

"So have you. And what have we done to deserve all this?"

He smiled but she continued to regard him soberly. "I really meant that."

"I know you did. Charming."

She began to put on her gloves. "I guess I'm just wasting your time, I'd better be going. You don't take me seriously."

"I don't take you seriously?" He raised his eyebrows. "Four people dead and I don't take you seriously? It's four now. The grand total. As you say, this *must* be the end of it. The finale — the climbing of a fence that can't be climbed, smash, bang, zowie."

"You needn't . . ."

"No, I needn't, but I will. She died a hideous death and one of you is responsible. You, or your father, or your brother, or your aunt. It's that simple, and that complicated. She wasn't killed cleanly, she was hounded to death. As by-products, there were two other deaths."

"You make us out a lovely family," she said dully. "Perfectly lovely. I'll be going now. Thanks for cheering me up, you and the calla lilies."

"It's not my business to cheer you up. Lieutenant Frome is at the Ford Hotel."

"What of it?"

"He seems a pleasant young man, though a little distraught. Having girl trouble. Once he's overseas I expect he'll forget about it."

She rose, drawing her coat close around her. "I've sent him back his ring. It would be useless to drag him into this mess. As you were kind enough to point out, it's a family matter and we'll keep it in the family."

"Why not let him decide that?"

"I make my own decisions and always have."

"Oh, sure. You have what is known as a lot of character, meaning you can be wrong at the top of your lungs." He got up and held out his hand to her across the desk. "Well, good-bye. It was nice seeing you."

She ignored his hand, recognizing the gesture as ironic. "Good-bye."

"See you at the funeral."

She paused on the way to the door and turned around. "Must you come?"

"Hell, I like funerals. I like to give my clients a good send-off. I'm having a wreath made: Happy Landing, Lucille."

Her face began to crumple and she put

out one hand as if to balance herself. "I have never — met — a more inhuman man."

"Inhuman?" He walked toward her slowly. "Do you realize that not one of you has given me a scrap of information to help me solve these murders? I might have saved Cora Green and your stepmother, and Eddy Greeley."

"Two insane people," she said in a bitter voice. "And a dope fiend. It was practically euthanasia. They were all old and hopeless. It's the young ones, Martin and me, who have to live on and suffer and never be able to forget or lead happy normal lives. It was Martin and me who had to live without a real mother. It was I who had to give up the only person I've ever really loved because I couldn't bear to have him disgraced too. Officers in the army can't afford to get mixed up in a scandal."

"That's his business."

"No, it's mine. If he lost his commission, all through our marriage every time we quarreled he would fling it up to me."

"If he's the flinging-up type he won't need any excuse."

"I didn't say he was that type! He isn't!"

"What you're saying is, that's what *you'd* do if you were he. Well, I'm not Dorothy Dix, I don't give a damn what you do as long as it doesn't come under homicide."

He thought she was on the verge of walking out and slamming the door. Instead she went back and sat down and took off her gloves again.

"All right," she said calmly. "What can I do to help you find out the truth?"

"Talk."

"About what?"

"It was on a Sunday, wasn't it, that you and your father and brother went to get Lieutenant Frome. And on Monday your stepmother ran away. Tell me everything that happened on those two days, what was said and who said it, even the most trivial things."

"I don't see how that will help."

"I do. Up to that point you were a fairly normal family group. You had made the adjustments to your real mother's death, and were living along with the normal trivial quarrels and jokes and affection . . ."

"That's not true. Not for me, anyway. I never adjusted to my mother's death and I had no affection for Lucille. I have never forgiven my father for marrying again."

"In any case you managed to live with her, like the rest, and even found her useful and competent sometimes, perhaps?"

"Yes."

"What I'm getting at is that something must have happened on that Sunday to precipitate matters. It doesn't look to me as if someone had been brooding for years about sending Lucille an amputated finger and waiting for a convenient train wreck. No, I think that on Sunday someone received a revelation, and the wreck itself suggested a means of getting back at Lucille."

"That leaves Edith out. She was at home."

"Yes."

"And that Sunday was just the same as other Sundays. I got up the same time as I always do and was the first one down for breakfast. Is that the sort of thing you want to hear?"

"Yes."

"Annie gave me orange juice and toast and coffee. The other maid, Della, was at church. Then Edith came down. She was a little fluttery about Giles coming and I remember she kept saying 'today of all days,' which annoyed me. I don't like fusses."

She paused. frowning thoughtfully down at her hands. "Oh, yes. Then father couldn't find something, as usual, and I heard Lucille talking up the stairs to him in the way she had — as if the rest of us were a bunch of children and she the well-trained nursemaid. She said something about trying the cedar closet and then she came in and had breakfast, and she and Edith talked. I expect Edith said the usual things to me, about my manners and my posture — she always did. After that Edith went up to get Martin and he came down and began to kid me about Giles. As soon as Martin came in Lucille left. I remember that because it was so pointed."

"Pointed?"

"Yes. Now that father and Edith weren't there she didn't have to put up with us and our chatter, she could get up and leave. When father was there she was all sweet and silky. No, I'm not being imaginative, either. You should have seen her face when I told her I was getting married. She positively beamed. One out, two to go, see? Perhaps Martin would get married too, and Edith might die, and then she could be alone with father. That's what she wanted. She never fooled Martin and me for an instant — even before . . ."

She stopped.

"Even before your mother died?" Sands said.

"Yes. Even then. She could hide it in front of grown-ups but not in front of us. Not that we were so perceptive and subtle, but because adults are so stupid about hiding things from children. They overdo it and you can smell the corn miles away. Well, that's why we didn't like her — because she was in love with my father. And she — stayed that way."

"And he?"

"Oh, he loved her," she said grudgingly. "Not in the same way that he loved my mother — Lucille was so different from her. Father always had to look after Mildred, but when he married Lucille she was the one who looked after him. She and Edith. Poor Father."

"Why poor?"

"Oh, I don't know. Because — well, I guess not many people understand my father. He's a very good doctor, there's no better gynecologist in the city. All day and half the night he'd be at his office or one of the hospitals or making his calls — very skillful and authoritative and all that — and then he'd come home and be gently and unobtrusively forced into taking aspirins and lying down for a rest and eating the right food. Sort of a schizophrenic existence. And all through it he's remained good-natured and kind and — well, a good egg. A couple of years ago Edith and Lucille pressed him into retiring from full practice. Maybe they were right, I don't know. He's never had very good health and a doctor's life is a hard one. Still — it's a thing for a man to settle by himself."

"Like marriage."

She flushed and said coldly, "That's different."

"All domineering women resent domineering women."

"A directly domineering woman is one thing, a sly managing female is another."

"Very feministic."

"And I didn't come here to argue."

"Then back to Sunday."

"I've told you everything. It was the most ordinary day in the world until we ran into the train wreck. From then on it became very confused. We all worked steadily until late that night. I hardly saw any of the others. I helped undress and wash the wounded and make beds and things like that. I haven't had much real hospital training, that's all I could do. I took time off to phone home because I knew Edith would be worried." Again the grudging note in her voice. "Lucille, too, I suppose, though not about us. That's really all I can tell you."

She got up, a stocky, healthy-looking girl with a direct and somewhat defiant gaze.

"I've talked too much," she said curtly,

pulling on her gloves.

"You've been very helpful."

"I — I'd rather you didn't tell the others I came here this morning. They wouldn't like it." She raised her head proudly. "Not that I'm in the least frightened."

"It might be wise to be a *little* frightened."

"If I admitted, in words, that I was even a little frightened, I'd never go home again."

She went out, the echo of her own words ringing in her ears: never go home again, never go home again.

But she could not resist a challenge, especially one that she presented to herself. And so she drove straight home.

She let herself in with her own key. As soon as the door opened she could smell the flowers, the heavy cloying calla lilies and the poisonously sweet carnations. Funeral flowers.

With Deepest Condolences — With Sincerest Sorrow.

Please omit flowers, the notice in the paper had read. But some of their friends thought a funeral just wasn't a funeral without flowers. And so they kept arriving by personal messengers and florist vans, to be unwrapped by Annie, and stacked up haphazardly in the living room by a distraught and red-eyed Edith.

"Idiots," Polly said through clenched teeth. "Idiots, idiots."

Edith came out of the living room. She looked old and tragic and she kept pressing one hand to her head as if to press away the pain.

"I'm so tired. I don't know what to do with all these flowers."

"Throw them out."

"It wouldn't look right. Someone might see us. It seems so silly, sending flowers when she isn't even here." Her words ended in a sob. "I have this blinding headache, I can't seem to think."

"Ask Father to give you something."

"No, I can't bother him. He didn't sleep all night."

The front door opened and Martin came in. A blast of cold air swept down the hall.

"Hello," Martin said cheerfully. "You've been out, Polly?"

Edith turned away and went quickly up the stairs without speaking to him.

Martin frowned at her back. "What's the matter with her lately? As soon as I come she goes."

"You get on her nerves, which doesn't surprise me. Give me a cigarette."

He tossed a package of cigarettes toward her. "Well, why do I get on her nerves?"

"Respect for the dead. That sort of thing."

"She's been doing this for two weeks. Lucille wasn't dead two weeks ago."

"If you're worried, why not ask her?"

"No, thanks. My policy is to stay away from the rest of the family as much as I can."

"Mine too," Polly said dryly. "And isn't that a coincidence?"

Martin looked at her with detachment. "Pretty long in the tooth and claw this morning, aren't you? Where have you been?"

"Here and there."

"Well, well." He looked amused but she could tell from the way his eyes narrowed that he was angry. "I don't seem to be much of a success with the ladies today. One walks out, the other shuts up."

"It's just pure envy. We'd like to be able to bury ourselves in books too."

"My work has to be done."

"Come hell or high water. You've made that clear."

"Oh, Lord." He put his hand out and caught her arm and smiled suddenly. "Look, there's no sense in the two of us fighting. We're the ones that have to stick together — aren't we?"

For a minute she couldn't speak. She felt

the tenseness in his voice and in his eyes, crinkled at the corners with smiling lines, yet cold because they were always turned in upon himself.

"Oh, sure," she said calmly, and shrugged away his hand. "We'll all stick together. There's not much else we can do."

"I'll be away this afternoon," Janet Green told her secretary. "See that these are ready for me in the morning and that Miss Lance gets the samples, and . . ." Her eyes settled vacantly on the desk. "Oh, that's all."

The secretary picked up the samples, frowning. Miss Green had been very absent-minded for the past few days. She was always forgetting things and breaking off sentences in the middle. In the secretary's opinion, Miss Green had been working too hard and should have had a holiday after the death of her sister.

As she passed across the front of the desk she gave Miss Green a sharp glance. Janet caught it.

"Damn," she muttered when the door closed. "I'll have to keep my mind on business. I shouldn't go there this afternoon. It's not my affair."

But it is, she answered herself silently. I have every right to go to her funeral; Cora died because of her.

Since she had read of Lucille's suicide in the paper, Janet's conscience had been troubling her. She felt that she had not done enough to help Lucille and that she was, in a sense, responsible for what happened. Twice she had begun to call Sands on the telephone seeking reassurance and explanations, but each time she had hung up again. Then the urge had seized her to go and see the Morrow family. She felt vaguely that once she had seen them, things would be clearer and the whole business less mysterious and frightening.

Since she did not want an actual encounter with the family she decided to go to the cemetery where Lucille was to be buried. There would be a crowd of curiosity-seekers there; no one would notice her.

But Janet's hope of remaining unnoticed was dispelled almost as soon as she arrived. Bad weather had kept most of the curiosity-seekers away; and to make it worse, she arrived late and the first person she saw was Sands.

He was standing apart from the little group of people clustered around the open grave. He had his hat off and the driving snow had whitened his hair. She began to walk around to the other side, conscious of the crunching noise her feet made in the snow.

He heard it, and looked up and nodded at her.

Janet hesitated and stood still. What bad taste to come here, she thought, what idiocy. If I could only get away quietly . . .

But it was too late, she couldn't get away. The minister was praying, and one of the group around the grave had turned around and was looking at her. It was an older woman, heavily draped in black, with a pale pinched face and dark tired eyes which said, without anger, without bitterness: *What are you doing here? Leave us alone.*

Ashes to ashes.

"Edith Morrow," Sands' voice said in her ear. Janet jumped. She hadn't heard him approaching and there was something sinister in the way he said, "Edith Morrow."

Dust to dust.

"Dr. Morrow's sister," Sands said. "Why did you come?"

"I wanted to see the Morrows."

"Well, there they are. Standing together, as usual. They do it well."

As if to disprove his statement, Edith Morrow turned and began walking toward them.

"You have no right to be here," she said to

Sands in her high desperate voice. "Trailing us even to the grave — despicable . . ." She made a nervous gesture with one black-gloved hand. "And these others — why did they come? Why can't they leave us alone?"

"This is Miss Green," Sands said quietly. "Cora Green's sister."

"C—Cora Green . . . ?"

Janet flushed. "I agree, I shouldn't have come. I'll leave immediately."

"It's all over anyway," Edith said harshly.

"I'm sorry. I thought of calling on you but then I'm a stranger to you."

"Why did you want to call?"

"Oh, I don't know. I thought I could help, perhaps. I met Mrs. Morrow at the hospital. . . ." She knew she was saying all the wrong things and turned to Sands for help. But he had slipped away. She couldn't see him anywhere.

She turned back and met Edith's gaze.

"I was rude," Edith said. "The apology should be mine."

"No, not at all."

"It was your sister who died?"

"Yes."

"We — one of us . . ."

"Oh, I don't look at it like that at all," Janet said in embarrassment. "I just thought

I'd — like to see you all."

"To judge us?"

"Yes, I suppose."

"You've seen us now." Edith leaned closer and her voice was a whisper. "Tell me, which one of us? Look at us and tell me, which *one* of us?"

There was a silence. Then Janet said, with warm deep sympathy, "You poor woman. It must be terrible for you!"

She no longer felt uncomfortable herself because here was someone who needed comforting.

"Mr. Sands could be wrong, you know," she said in her rich voice. "Policemen often are. Very likely it'll turn out that he's been far too imaginative, and some day perhaps you'll all be laughing about how suspicious you were of each other."

"If I could think that . . ."

"Well, I *do* think it. We're all inclined to take things too seriously, all except Cora. She was a great laugher. Sometimes when I'm alone at night and feeling mopey I remember some of the jokes she made and get to laughing myself. I haven't any real friends, you know, there was just Cora."

"Nor have I."

"I've always been too busy to make friends, and now when I could use some I don't know how to go about it."

"I wouldn't know either," Edith said. She was astonished to find herself talking so personally and at such an odd time to a total stranger. The wind had whipped a little color to her cheeks, and she felt her rigid neck relaxing and the hard dry lump in her throat dissolving. She had stepped temporarily outside the walls of her own world and was reluctant to go back. They were waiting for her, she knew, but she kept her eyes fixed deliberately on Janet, a stranger, and so one who could be trusted.

"What do you do?" Edith said. "I mean, suppose you want to have a — a good time, what do you do?"

"Oh, I dress all up and take myself to dinner," Janet said, smiling. "And then to a concert or a movie, perhaps."

"I'd like that."

"There's no reason why we couldn't go together some time."

"You wouldn't mind having me along?"

"I'd like it very much. We could get really silly and buy a bottle of champagne."

"Do you ever do that?"

"Once. I felt very frivolous and giggled through a whole performance of *Aïda*."

Champagne, Edith thought, a gay giddy drink, for weddings, for youth, not for two lonely aging women . . .

"Yes, I'd like that," she said, without hope. "I guess — they're waiting for me. I'd better go."

"No, wait. I really mean it, about having dinner together. We'll make it a definite day."

"Any day. They're all the same."

"How about next Tuesday?"

"Tuesday. That would be fine."

"I could meet you in the Arcadian Court and we'll go to see *The Doughgirls* if you like."

She had the uncomfortable feeling that Edith was no longer listening to her, that the two of them had, in a few minutes, gone through the emotional experience of months or years — from antagonism through friendship to mutual boredom.

"See you Tuesday then," she said with extra heartiness to compensate for her thoughts. "In the meantime don't worry too much. We and our troubles aren't so important as we think." She laid her hand for an instant on Edith's arm. "Good-bye and good luck."

"Good-bye," Edith said, and turned and stepped back into her own world.

Janet's eyes followed her, full of pity and understanding. The little group beside the grave was waiting for her. When Edith had almost reached them she stumbled and the younger man put out his hand to steady her. Edith shrank away from him and pulled the black veil down over her face.

It was only a gesture, yet Janet felt ashamed to have witnessed it. She walked quickly back to her car.

On the way home she began to make further plans for Tuesday. Perhaps the Arcadian Court was too stuffy. They might try Angelo's if Edith liked spaghetti — or some place down in the village where you saw such queer people, sometimes. . . .

By the time she got home she had everything planned, but she never saw Edith again.

CHAPTER 12

"Who was that?" Martin said.

"A friend of mine," Edith replied, pressing her lips together tightly behind the veil. "Someone you don't know."

"In brief, none of my business?"

"Exactly."

"All right. I was just trying to be pleasant."

He opened the car door and she got in the back seat. She was breathing fast, as if she was excited.

"You should take it easier, Edith," Andrew said, and sat down beside her and shut the door. "There's no hurry. Is there?"

"No."

He raised his voice. "Martin, you might stop and pick up some cigarettes some place." He spoke easily and naturally, as master of the house setting the tone and pace for a new set of circumstances.

Edith looked at him gratefully and covered his hand with hers. "That was kind of you, Andrew."

He professed not to understand. "What was?"

"Oh, you know, just being ordinary."

He closed his eyes wearily. "I'm always ordinary."

"No, I mean . . ."

"Now don't be silly, Edith."

They fell into a companionable silence while in the front seat Polly and Martin discussed a book he was reviewing.

At the first drugstore Martin stopped the car and got out to buy the cigarettes. When he came out of the store he was whistling, but as soon as he saw the car he became silent and adjusted his face self-consciously as if he'd just caught sight of himself in a mirror, wearing the wrong expression.

It was a small thing and no one noticed it but Edith. Behind the veil her eyes glittered. Martin flung her a mocking glance and slid behind the wheel.

We watch each other, she thought.

The phrase echoed in her mind. *We watch each other.* Someone had said that recently. Who was it?

She remembered with a shock that she herself had written it to Lucille. It was the first time she'd thought of the letter since she'd sent it, and she flushed with shame at her own stupidity. She should never have written it. Where was it now? Destroyed, surely. But suppose it wasn't destroyed?

Suppose it was in the bundle of clothes and things that the hospital had sent back this morning?

Her mind set up a wild clamor: I must get the letter, Andrew mustn't see it — no one . . .

As soon as they arrived home she excused herself with a headache and went upstairs. She had intended to go straight to Lucille's room to look for the bundle and make sure the letter had been destroyed. But Annie was in the hall vacuuming the rug.

When Annie saw her she shut off the motor and the vacuum bag deflated with a drawn-out whine.

"This isn't the time to be doing the rugs, is it?" Edith said.

Annie looked surprised, and a little sulky. "Maybe not, but I figured I might as well be doing something if you wouldn't let me go to the funeral." She was gratified to note that her subtle counter-attack made Edith ill at ease, and she pressed her advantage. "If it wouldn't be too much trouble, Miss Morrow, I figured you'd look at the food grinder in the kitchen. It's not working and Della accuses me of losing one of the parts which I never did."

"Some other time — not now."

"Well, I just thought, I was just thinking

I needed it to make the stuffing for the veal."

I'll teach you, her eyes said, for keeping me away from the funeral of someone who had more class than all the rest of you put together.

"I just thought it'd be nice," she said blankly. "You can't buy food grinders any more."

"All right, I'll see it," Edith said.

She passed the door of Lucille's room without looking at it, and went down the stairs again with Annie following her. She had a sudden wild notion that Annie had opened the bundle from the hospital and seen the letter, that she must be placated.

"About Mrs. Morrow's clothes," she said, and tried to keep the agitation out of her voice.

"I put them in Dr. Morrow's room," Annie said. "Naturally he'll want to look over it, I figured. I didn't touch a thing."

"I didn't say you had."

"Over here's the grinder. See? Here's where the screw's missing."

Edith bent over it. Her body drooped with weariness, it seemed that it would never have the strength to right itself again.

"It's so — so complicated," she whispered.

"If Mrs. Morrow was here, she'd know about it. She was real handy around the house."

"I'm sorry, I . . ."

"You look real bad, Miss Morrow. Maybe you'd like a cup of tea? You go up and lie down and I'll bring you a cup of tea. I don't really *have* to stuff the veal."

Then why didn't you say so? Edith screamed silently, why didn't you say so?

"It's just as nice *not* stuffed," Annie said. "The tea'll be up in a jiffy."

"Thank you," Edith said, and turned, and dragged herself back up the stairs. There was no use arguing with Annie, and no use getting excited. The letter wasn't important. It was probably not there anyway, and even if it was, there was nothing in it except a record of her own fears and her own folly.

I'll see about it later on, she thought, and lay down on her bed, with one arm shielding her eyes from the light.

Annie brought the tea in and left again. Edith lay without moving. She could feel her migraine coming on, the beat of the blood on one side of her neck and up along the artery behind the ear. Pretty soon the actual pain would be there, and after that the nausea. She began to massage the side of her neck gently, the way Andrew had told her to do when she felt the first symptom.

But it was no use. By dinnertime the pain was intense, and immediately after dinner she came back to her room and lay listening to the sounds that filtered through the house, Annie and Della washing up in the kitchen and then going up to their rooms on the third floor. A little later they came down again, whispering, and the back door opened and closed.

They're going to a movie, Edith thought and remembered Janet Green and Tuesday, and the funeral, and then the letter again.

In the darkness she got off the bed and crept to the door and out into the hall. She could hear people talking down in the living room, and she waited until she could distinguish all their voices, Polly's and Martin's and Andrew's, so she would know she was alone upstairs.

She hesitated, suddenly appalled by her own secretiveness. Why, they were her own family, down there. And she, herself, had every right to go into Andrew's room and sort out Lucille's clothes — every right, it was her duty, in fact, she must spare Andrew — there was no need to be afraid.

But in silence and in secret her slippered feet crossed the hall. It was only when she had switched on a lamp in Andrew's room that some of her fear left her. For the room was like Andrew himself, it was familiar and comfortable and getting old, but it had worn well. Even the smell was reassuring — polished leather and books and tobacco.

She glanced toward the smoking stand beside the leather chair and saw that Andrew had left the lid of the humidor off. Automatically she walked over and replaced it. His pipe lay across the ash tray, and an open book straddled one arm of the chair.

He must have been up all night, she thought. Walking around and smoking and trying to read and then pacing the room again. She felt suddenly overwhelmed with pity for him and her knees sagged against the chair.

The book slid limply to the floor. It made only a faint noise, yet she went rigid, and a trickle of ice water seemed to ooze down her spine. Her ears moved a little, like an animal's waiting for some sound, some signal . . .

But there was no sound. Hurriedly she bent to pick up the book. It was a diary.

Funny, I didn't know Andrew kept a diary, she thought. No, it can't be his. The writing's different, very round and big, and the ink's faded. I mustn't look at it . . . None of my business . . . I must find my letter. . . .

She closed the book and put it on the arm of the chair again. She had already turned to walk away before the name on the cover penetrated to her mind.

Then she became aware that someone was walking along the hall outside. The blood pounded against her ears, and unconsciously she began to rub her neck.

"What are you doing in here, Edith?" Andrew said, and the door clicked in place behind him.

Her hand paused. "I — I was looking for Lucille's clothes."

"They're in the closet. We thought you were asleep."

"No — no — I — couldn't sleep."

She saw his eyes go toward the chair and falter.

"I didn't read it," she said. "It fell, I just picked it up. But I didn't read it."

"Don't talk like a child. What difference would it make if you had read it?" He closed his eyes for a second. "Mildred never wrote anything that other people couldn't see."

"You read it — last night?"

"Yes."

"You've kept it all these years?"

"All these years, yes."

Her hand began to move again up and down the cord of her neck. "But I thought

— wasn't it missing after she died? Didn't the policeman . . . ?"

"Yes, it was missing. I had it. I didn't feel justified in handing my wife's diary over to a policeman. You were the one who told the police that the only things missing after she died were the jewels she had on and her diary?"

"Yes, I told them, I was the one."

"Silly of you, Edith," he said gently. "Did you think there might be a clue in it?"

"Perhaps — for a while . . ."

He picked up the book and handed it to her. "Take it with you."

"No, no, I wouldn't want to read it! It will just upset me. . . . I have this headache."

"It won't upset you. It's a very ordinary diary, just the little things that happened to her day by day, about the children, and us."

He was still holding the book out to her and now she took it, almost without volition.

"Don't show it to the children," he said. "They're not old enough yet to get any comfort from the past."

"You look tired," Edith said with a return of her old crispness. "You'd better go to bed."

"I'll sit up and smoke for awhile."

"You have to take better care of yourself,

Andrew, keep more regular hours. I noticed you didn't touch your salad tonight."

"Don't nag, Edith."

"I wasn't nagging."

"Go to bed yourself."

"I would, if I could sleep," she said gratingly. "You'll never give me anything to make me sleep."

"It's a bad habit."

"It can't be a habit if you do it once!" She knew that she was getting shrill and tried to stop herself, but too many things had happened to her today — the funeral, Janet, the diary, the migraine — she felt her control slipping away. "Other doctors give sleeping prescriptions! I'm your own sister and I have to lie awake night after night . . ."

"You're the type who forms habits too easily," he said quietly. "But rather than see you hysterical like this I will set aside my better judgment."

Even though she was getting her own way she couldn't stop talking at him. Her voice pursued him into the closet where he kept his medical supplies locked up, and into the bedroom where he poured out a glass of water.

"Here. Take this. It will begin to work in an hour or so. Now go to bed."

He half-pushed her toward the door, glad

to be rid of her finally, to be able to enjoy the peace and darkness of his own room.

At ten o'clock the maids came home, and went, twittering, up to the third floor. Shortly afterward Martin came to bed, and last of all, Polly. She had locked the house and put out the lights, and now she paused in front of Edith's door and rapped softly.

"Who is it?"

"Me. Polly."

"Oh. I'm in bed."

"I saw your light on."

"Well, come in. Don't shout at me through the door!"

Edith was sitting up in bed. Her cheeks were flushed and her eyes had a glaring sightless look. She wore a bed-jacket.

"I was just sitting here a moment before turning off the light," she said.

One of her arms jerked nervously and the sleeve of the bed-jacket slid back and showed an inch or so of the black dress she'd been wearing. She covered it again quickly, but Polly had already seen.

"Well, I didn't have anything special to say," she said, her voice carefully blank. "Guess I'll turn in. How's your headache?"

"Headache? Oh, it's all right."

"Well, good night."

"Good night."

Their eyes met for an instant and passed on, like strangers on a dark street.

The door closed and Edith got out of bed and tore the bed-jacket from her shoulders. She put on a coat and tied a black scarf over her head and picked up the diary from underneath the bedclothes.

Then, a black shadow, she moved through the house, and went out into the street.

CHAPTER 13

"Good morning, Mr. Bascombe," D'arcy said. "Mr. Sands has just come in. I was terribly sorry to hear you're leaving us."

Bascombe stopped, looked him up and down. "Yeah, I know."

"We were all thrilled to hear you got a commission. I bet you'll look swell in your uniform."

"Ask me to take it off for you some time and see where it gets you."

D'arcy looked pained. "That's no way to talk. I thought you'd be nice to me at least on your last day."

Smiling grimly, Bascombe strode into Sands' office.

Sands looked up and said, "Good morning. How's the Military Intelligence this morning?"

Bascombe saluted smartly. "I beg to report, sir, that A-56 of the Division of Lawns and Gardens, that is, myself, has discovered the existence of a pansy in your own office. A-56 recommends fertilization of the roots or complete extermination."

Sands laughed. "Sit down. When do you leave?"

"It's a military secret, even from me."

"Ellen back?"

"Yeah. She's pulling the gag about how-can-I-live-without-you-my-hero. I've signed the papers for her allotment, now I'm forgetting the whole thing." He sat on the edge of the desk, swinging one foot. "I hope."

"Got the jitters?"

"Some. Afraid I'll pull a boner. What I've been doing around here seems like kid stuff compared to what's in store for me."

"I don't think you have to be afraid. D'arcy says you have a *truly great* brain."

"What the hell!" Bascombe swung himself off the desk embarrassed. "Well, good-bye." He held out his hand. "It's been damn nice having a decent guy in this dump."

Sands, too, was embarrassed. He got up, and they shook hands across the desk. "Good-bye and good hunting."

"Thanks."

Bascombe went out. In the outer office he saw D'arcy talking to a middle-aged woman. He noticed the woman especially because she was carrying an enormous leather handbag.

Well — what the hell — women, to hell with them . . .

"There now," D'arcy said to the woman.

"Now you can go in."

She seemed distraught. "Thank you. I — it's really urgent."

"Just step in." D'arcy opened the door of Sands' office with a flourish. "Miss Green to see you, sir."

"Good morning, Miss Green," Sands said, and was surprised to see how agitated she looked. "What brings you here?"

"I can't make head nor tail of it. Look." She opened the big handbag and drew out a paper bag.

"Shut that door, D'arcy."

"Oh, yes, sir."

Janet Green put the paper bag on the desk. It had been stamped and postmarked, and Janet Green's name and address had been written shakily in pen and ink.

"I just don't know what to make of it," she said. "This came this morning, a while ago. It's a diary, and why anyone should send me a diary . . ."

Sands took the book carefully from the bag. The cover was tooled leather and across it, in gold letters, was printed "Mildred Scott Morrow." He opened it. The ink was faded but still legible. "July 3, 1928. Today is my birthday and Edith has given me this lovely diary. I told her, what would *I* put in a diary, I never have anything interesting to say . . ."

"Why to *me?*" Janet cried in exasperation. "I thought, of course, as soon as I saw the name Morrow that Edith Morrow herself must have sent it. I don't know any of the others at all. And yet I only met her yesterday."

"Perhaps that's why."

"What is?"

"She could trust you because you have no ax to grind."

"Yes, but there's nothing in the book that I can see! And why not keep it herself? The strange thing is that someone has marked passages in it here and there. They're mostly about Lucille."

"Go on."

"Well, as soon as I looked into the book I rang up Edith Morrow. At least I rang the house and whoever answered the phone sounded very peculiar. They said that Miss Morrow couldn't come to the phone. Then they hung up, just like that."

Before she had finished speaking Sands had risen. "Thanks for coming. I'll keep this. I'm in a hurry."

"You can't leave me . . ."

"Sorry. D'arcy will see you out. I've got to leave."

He went to the coat rack and slipped the

diary into the pocket of his overcoat. Then with the coat over his arm he walked out.

When he reached the Morrow house the doorbell was answered by Annie.

She recognized him and said, "Oh!" and put her hand over her mouth.

"I'd like to speak to Miss Edith Morrow," he said.

"Well, you can't."

"Why not?"

"She's dead. And it's none of your business this time. It happened natural. She died in her sleep."

She opened the door a little wider, not wide enough for him to walk in comfortably, but just enough so that he could squeeze through the opening if he really had the nerve to come calling on people at a time like this. . . .

"I'm very sorry," he said, and Annie was impressed by his sincerity. Her face lost its guarded look.

"I've been real miserable about it," she said. "I wasn't very nice to her yesterday and now I'll never have a chance to make it up to her. That's the first thing I thought of when I found her this morning. There she was lying on the bed, all stiff and peaceful, and I thought, now it's too late, now I'll never have a chance to make it up to her."

"Where is the family?"

"They're up there with her."

"I don't want to intrude on them." Too late now. Edith was stiff and peaceful, at home with her family. "I'll wait some place. Don't bother telling them I'm here. I'll just wait."

"They wouldn't like it if I didn't tell them. They don't like having a policeman around. There's a fire in Dr. Morrow's den, you can go in there, I guess, but I don't really think they'll like it."

"I'll take a chance."

She left him then, and when he heard her go upstairs he took the diary from his coat pocket and began to read.

In the first few pages there was nothing marked, no reference to Lucille. Mildred Morrow had been chiefly concerned with her family and the details of the home. He read at random:

August 4.

Raining today and Polly is pestering me to let her get her curls cut off. I suppose I'm old-fashioned, I don't really want her to do it. But if I say no she'll just go to Andrew and twist him around her little finger. What a Daddy's girl she is! I told Andrew, it's a shame he can't see more of his children. But then he is doing so *much good* for the world I feel selfish.

August 31.

Edith looks so pretty today! She's got on a new dress, so I told her, we must do something *special. So* we had a picnic in the park! Lucille came along. I think Lucille could be very beautiful if she would only have some vitality. (Like Edith) She is still far too young to go on grieving for her husband. He was a lot older than she, and what we saw of him, not a nice person like her. The children came on the picnic too but they don't seem to like Lucille. She is too shy.

The last sentence was underlined in fresh ink.

September 6.

Well, I finally got Lucille and Andrew together! Andrew had a *whole evening off,* and though we've been Lucille's neighbors for ages, why, Andrew hardly knows her he's away so much! We played cards *(not* bridge!) and I told Andrew, here you are with three women, after seeing women all day you must be tired of them. He said no, they whetted his appetite, and we all laughed.

In the entries for the next two months there were various short references to Lucille.

We went shopping today. Lucille doesn't buy much, which puzzles me, because she certainly needs clothes.

I am getting very fond of Lucille. Once you know her she is really delightful, though Andrew and Edith don't believe me! Martin is getting to that smart-alecky stage and he calls Lucille "the blondy." Martin is very *hard* to handle. Though he's awfully good in his studies I think he's very sensitive about not being able to join in games and things since he had his back broken. Lucille says he is "compensating," whatever that means. She is much cleverer than I am.

Much cleverer, Sands thought. Far too clever for you, Mildred. He felt a strange pity for this woman who had been dead for sixteen years and had come to life again on paper, in all her guilelessness and sweet stupidity.

November 12.

I started my Christmas shopping today and tonight Edith went to her club and Andrew is working, of course. So I am sitting in Lucille's living room writing this while she knits. She knits with her eyes shut, imagine! I asked her what she was thinking and she told me that she was thinking she wasn't going to celebrate Christmas this year. Not celebrate Christmas! I told her, why not? She was very annoyed for a minute. She told me, look around you, look at my house and my clothes, can't you figure it out by yourself? Well, of course I could *then.* It was very embarrassing and I asked her if she wanted some money, a loan or a gift or *anything.* But she refused. I think she refused on account of Andrew, she knows he doesn't much like her.

December 2.

Polly found out today (isn't that just like her! She is a minx!) that Lucille's car, which we all thought was stored in her garage, has really been sold.

December 4.

I took my portrait down to Morison's for a good cleaning today. Lucille came along and afterward we went to a movie and then to Child's for a cup of chocolate (which I should *not* drink). She is so quiet and patient, it's nice to go places with her. Edith is always in so much of a hurry!

Quiet and patient, Sands thought. Biding her time, thinking out the plan that was, in the end, to destroy not only Mildred and herself, but three others. How did the plan start? At what particular moment did she begin to covet Mildred's husband and Mildred's money?

December 5.

Well, here I am over at Lucille's again tonight. I told her, this is getting to be practically a tradition! But it is nice (and *I mean* it!) to have someone to drop in on after the children are in bed and when Andrew is on a case and Edith is out. Edith is having quite a rush from this George Mackenzie, but Lucille says she doesn't think Edith will marry him because she's too wrapped up in Andrew. I was quite surprised at this! I mean, I know Edith *adores* Andrew and harries the life out of him, but I always thought it's because she hasn't a man of her own. I told Lucille this and she just smiled. But I still think I'm *right!* You don't know everything, I told her, just in fun, of course!

Sands had nearly reached the end now, and with each page he turned, the picture of Mildred became clearer. Mildred, smiling and secure, never questioning, never looking behind her to see the inexorable fate that was creeping up on her. Happy Mildred, proud of her husband and his work, secure in the knowledge that her life was to be a series of repetitions, of Andrew and Edith, and the children and new dresses and cups of chocolate; and, like a child herself, never tiring of repetitions.

December 7.

Lucille and I took a walk through the park this afternoon. We talked about marriage. I guess it started when I said something about how attractive Andrew was to women. My goodness, every once in a while one of them makes a big scene at his office and poor Andrew is so completely bewildered by the whole thing. He considers himself an old fogy. At thirty-four! Anyway, I told Lucille this and for some reason she lost her reserve and began to talk about her own marriage. Both her parents died in a hotel fire when she was seventeen, and quite soon afterward she married one of her father's friends, years older than she was. She said she hated him from the very first day. (And the way she said it! I couldn't believe it was really my own friend talking!) Imagine living in hate for ten years! No wonder it's left its mark on her. I *do* wish she would let me help her in some way. You really should get married again, I told her.

December 10.

I bought Lucille's Christmas present today, a gorgeous rawhide dressing case, and of course now Polly wants one too. Andrew phoned to say he won't be home until late tonight because Mrs. Peterson's time is up and she absolutely refuses to go to a hospital. So I guess I'll drop over to Lucille's for a while. I want to show her the new earrings Andrew bought me. Later. Well, here I am. Lucille has the living room beautifully decorated for Christmas with clusters of pine tied with ribbon. I was quite envious. I asked her where she got it and she said she'd simply gone out into the park and cut it, and we both laughed. I think I'll try it too! The pine smells so fresh and clean, and think of the fun cutting it for oneself!

It was the last entry. The pictures kept forming in Sands' mind, though there were no more words to hang them on.

Mildred, pink and pretty against the pine.

"Oh, I love it! It smells so fresh and clean."

"Yes, doesn't it. I cut it myself."

"How exciting!"

"We could go out and cut some for you. It's

snowing, the night is dark, and I have an ax."

"An ax? Oh, goody!"

"Yes, an ax . . ."

Had the details of the plan occurred to her suddenly at that point? Or had she plotted it carefully beforehand, using the pine as the bait for Mildred to swallow, more innocent than any trout? No one would ever know now. Lucille's secrets had been buried with her in a closed coffin.

They went, laughing, out into the snow.

"Oh, this is fun! Wait'll I tell Andrew."

"Here, let me cut it for you. I'm bigger than you are."

"Do be careful. It's rather frightening out here alone, isn't it?"

"I'm not frightened."

"I just meant, the dark. I can hardly see you, Lucille! Lucille! Where are you? Lucille!"

"Why, I'm right here. Behind you. With an ax."

The ax swung and whistled. The snow fell soundlessly and covered Mildred and the tracks.

What had Lucille done with the ax? Put it in the furnace, Sands thought. The handle would burn, and if the fire was high enough the blade itself might be distorted beyond recognition. And Mildred's jewels — had she put them in the furnace with the ax, or did she hide them, hoping to sell them later? Perhaps she had never intended to sell them and had taken them only in the hope that Mildred's death would be construed as a robbery.

As it was, Sands thought grimly. Thanks to Inspector Hannegan's precious bungling.

He returned to Lucille. He could see her destroying the ax, and hiding the jewels and then coming, suddenly, upon the diary Mildred had left behind in the sitting room. If she hadn't been pressed for time she might have read the diary then and there and realized that it would have to be destroyed. But she didn't have time to read it if it should prove harmless to her.

Where has it been all these years? Sands thought.

At one o'clock Andrew Morrow had come home.

"Edith! Edith, wake up! Mildred isn't home yet. Something must have happened to her."

"Why, she was just over at Lucille's."

"I'm going over to get her."

They had gone over to Lucille's but they didn't get Mildred.

"She left here ages ago, before eleven o'clock. I thought she was going straight home."

"She's not there."

"She may have decided to go for a walk,

and stumbled and fell."

"Come on, Edith, we'll look for her."

"Wait and I'll get dressed and help you look."

She had helped them look, guiding them firmly away from the tree that sheltered Mildred.

Hers had remained the guiding hand. She soothed Edith and nursed Andrew through his illness and got the children off to school; and when she had become indispensable, he married her.

Sands closed the diary and put it in his pocket. He thought of Edith creeping downstairs with the diary, finding only a paper bag to wrap it in, and sending it not to him, Sands, but to her new friend, Janet Green.

To send it to me would have been too final and definite an act, he thought. She wasn't sure, she wanted only to get the diary in some safe place outside the house until she could decide what to do about it.

He felt a sudden terrible pity for Edith, not because she was dead but because in her childish impulsiveness and indecision she had sent the diary to Janet Green.

Polly came in and found Sands slumped in the chair, holding his head with one hand.

He rose when he saw her, but for a minute neither of them spoke. He noticed that she had not been crying but her face had the strained set look that told of deep and bitter tears inside.

"I was — we were just going to phone you. My father will be down in a minute. He thinks — he thinks Edith killed herself."

"Why?" Sands said, and had to repeat it. "Why?"

"It wasn't natural." She turned her face and gazed stonily out of the window. "My father thinks it was morphine."

"Why morphine?"

"I don't know. He just thinks so. She was in his room last night, half-hysterical, begging him to give her something to make her sleep. He unlocked his cupboard and then went into the bathroom to mix her a bromide. It must have been then when it happened."

"What did?"

"When she — took the morphine."

"Why?"

She turned and looked at him. "You keep asking why and I don't know."

"Can you take advice?"

"I don't know what you mean."

"Get out of this house right away. Walk out the door and don't look back."

"Are you — crazy?"

"Go to your lieutenant. Don't stop to pack or think. Pick up your coat and get out."

"I — can't."

"Don't argue."

Her eyes widened. "I don't understand you. You're frightening me. I can't leave my father. And there's no reason — no reason . . ."

He reached out and grasped her shoulder savagely.

"Get out of this house. Run. Don't let anything stop you."

Neither of them had heard Andrew approaching. He spoke from the doorway. "Mr. Sands is right. I advise you to go."

He sounded tired but perfectly under control. "Lieutenant Frome's leave is up Sunday, isn't it? Today is Thursday, you haven't much time."

She looked from one man to the other, her mouth open in bewilderment.

"I don't understand. You know I can't leave you here alone, Father."

"Why not? Has it occurred to you that I might prefer to be alone?"

Sands stepped back and watched the two of them. It might have been an ordinary family argument except that the girl's eyes had too much fear in them, and there was too much acid in the man's voice.

"I think I'm old enough to be allowed some freedom, Polly. Edith is dead now, the whole business is ended. Do you know what that means to me, in plain realistic terms? It means I'm no longer phone-ridden."

The girl's face moved, and it seemed for an instant as if she was going to cry or laugh at the ridiculous word.

"It means," he said, "that wherever I choose to go, at whatever time, I won't be required to phone home and give my exact location, the nature of my companions, and the state of my health. I am now a free agent, an emancipated man. I've had to suffer to get to this point but I'm there now. *Nothing whatever is expected of me.*"

"I'm not the type who interferes," Polly said. She tried to sound cold and scornful but her voice trembled. "I don't require ten-minute reports, you wouldn't have to be phone-ridden. I'm not — I'm not Edith."

"No. But Edith wasn't always Edith either. Years ago Edith too was engaged to a young man. But when Mildred died she broke her engagement, she said it was her duty to stay with me. The fact was that she didn't love the young man enough to take a chance on marriage, so she eased herself out of it by that word *duty*. As the years passed Edith closed her mind to the real facts. She blamed me for her frustrated love affair. She took it out on me, not overtly, but by kind and gentle and loving nagging."

She looked at him, stubborn and mute.

"I'm wasting my time pointing out analogies. I'll have to give you a direct order, Polly. Leave this house."

"I won't. This is ridiculous."

"Leave this house immediately, do you hear?"

"You might at least keep your voice down. The maids . . ."

He saw that she had no intention of going. Even though she might have wanted to, her own obstinacy was in the way.

"I'm sorry," he said, and struck her on the cheek with the flat of his hand.

Her face seemed to break apart under the blow. With a sudden whimper she turned and ran out of the room holding her hand to her cheek.

The two men stood in silence. They heard the front door open and slam shut, a car engine racing, the blast of a horn, and then just quiet again.

"I'm sorry," Andrew repeated. "I — I don't really believe in violence."

"No," Sands said. "It boomerangs."

"The poor child, she was frightened to death."

"She'll get over it. Edith won't."

"Edith — yes. You want to see Edith, of course?"

"Yes."

"Very peaceful. Morphine is a peaceful death. You go to sleep, you dream, you never know where the dream ends."

Where the dream ends — for Greeley in an alley and Edith in her soft bed.

CHAPTER 14

She had not undressed. She lay on the bed, a blanket covering her to the waist, her head resting easily on two pillows.

"She didn't go to bed," Andrew said softly, as if she might wake at any minute and be displeased to find him in her bedroom talking about her. "She wouldn't have liked to be found in a nightgown."

"You think that's it?"

"Perhaps. I'm only guessing. It's all we can do now."

Sands moved closer to the bed. Edith's hands were folded and he saw that one of her fingers had a smudge of ink on it. His eyes strayed to the night table beside the bed. It held a glass of water and a pitcher and a lamp. At the base of the lamp lay a fountain pen with the top jammed carelessly on.

Sands thought, she sat here marking the passages in the diary. She worked quickly — why? Was she fighting against time, or was she in a hurry to go to sleep, to dream, to die?

"Why?" he said aloud. Why go to all the

trouble of marking the diary and seeing that it got in neutral and therefore safe hands?

"Why kill herself?" Andrew said, quietly. "Because she'd written a letter. When I came upstairs last night she was in my room trying to find it. It was in the bundle of Lucille's clothes that came from the hospital. She was afraid that I might read it and find out that she had driven Lucille to suicide."

"I see."

"Here it is. I read it last night."

He brought the letter from his pocket and handed it to Sands.

Sands read the agitated scrawl:

"Dear Lucille: I hope you received the chocolates and pillow rest I sent day before yesterday. It is very difficult to get chocolates these days, one has to stand in line. We all miss you a great deal, though I feel so hopeless saying it because I know you won't believe it. Everything is such a mess. The policeman Sands was here again, talking about the train wreck. You remember that afternoon? I don't know what he was getting at, but whoever did anything to you, Lucille, it wasn't me, Lucille, it was not me! I don't know, I can't figure anything out any more. I have this sick headache nearly all the time and Martin is driving me crazy.

They have always seemed like my own children to me, the two of them, and now, I don't know, I look at them and they're like strangers. Meals are the worst time. We watch each other. That doesn't sound like much but it's terrible — we watch each other. I know Andrew wouldn't like me to be writing a letter like this. But, Lucille, you're the only one I can talk to now. I feel I'd rather be there with you, I've always liked and trusted you. Everything is so mixed up. Do you remember the night Giles came and I said, God help me, that we were a happy family? I feel this is a judgment on me for my smugness and wickedness. I don't know how it will all end. Edith."

It had all ended now, for both of them. Edith's calm cold face denied all knowledge. *Whoever did anything to you, Lucille, it wasn't me, Lucille, it was not me!* Those words rang clear and true in Sands' mind.

"She had to get the letter back," Andrew said. "She knew that Lucille killed herself soon after it was read to her, and she realized that if other people read it they would know the letter was mainly responsible for Lucille's death."

Sands barely heard him. He was looking at Edith, seeing the cold denial on her face.

The diary felt large and heavy in his pocket, as if it had grown since he'd put it there.

He turned suddenly and walked back to the door. The diary swung against his side, and when he passed Andrew he saw Andrew's eyes on his coat pocket.

"Do you carry a gun?" Andrew said.

"No."

"What's that?"

"A book."

"If you don't carry a gun, what do you do in an emergency?"

"I plan for emergencies. Then they are no longer emergencies." He smiled, very faintly. "Do *you* carry a gun?"

"No."

"You are against violence, I had forgotten. Excuse me, I have to phone in a report. Your sister — must be attended to."

"Yes, of course. You know where the phone is."

Sands was gone for ten minutes. When he came back Andrew was standing in the hall outside Edith's room, waiting for him.

"That book in your pocket," he said, "that's my wife's diary, isn't it?"

"Yes."

"I thought it would be. I couldn't find it. I gave it to Edith last night to read."

"Why?"

"She found it in my room when she came to look for her letter. I thought it was the natural thing to do, to let her read it."

"Natural," Sands repeated. "Everything's been pretty natural all down the line, hasn't it? Everything has more or less just *happened.*"

"I'm glad you see that. I feel it very strongly myself."

"Yes, I know."

"The only really unnatural thing is where you got my wife's diary."

"Your sister wrapped it in a paper bag and mailed it to Janet Green last night before she died." Seeing Andrew's frown he added, "She was at the funeral yesterday. Cora Green's sister."

"Oh, yes. The little old woman who ate the grapes." He flung a quick uncertain glance at Sands. "Well, at least nobody could claim that was anything but an accident."

"Nobody has."

"And Lucille herself, and the Greeley fellow, and now Edith — all accidents."

"If you plan accidents," Sands said grimly, "then they are no longer accidents."

Andrew laughed. "Ah, yes. Like the emergency." He sobered at the look on Sands' face. He felt that he must somehow deflect that cold direct gaze. "What were we talking about?"

"Accidents."

"And the diary, yes. I didn't imagine Edith would do anything so preposterous as sending it to Janet Green."

"Why did you give her the diary to read?"

"I told you, she found it in my room, I thought she would be interested in it."

"No. I think you were making one of your experiments. On Edith's mind, this time. When you first read the diary it threw you completely. You wanted to see what it would do to Edith."

"When I first read the diary?" Andrew repeated. "Why, I've had it for years, as I told Edith."

"But once she'd read it she didn't believe you. Any more than I do. I think you found the diary two weeks ago last Sunday."

They were both silent. The words spun between them — two weeks ago last Sunday — and Sands could picture Polly sitting in his office yesterday morning, saying blankly: "It was the most ordinary Sunday . . . Father couldn't find something, as usual, his scarf, I think it was. . . ."

"You couldn't have had the diary all this time," Sands said, "without knowing that Lucille had killed your first wife. And having that knowledge you could never have lived with her for fifteen years. It is humanly impossible."

A door opened at the end of the hall and Martin came out. Though he walked slowly Sands had the impression that he was holding himself back, that if he thought no one was looking he would bound along the hall, as buoyant and unfeeling as an animal.

"Oh, there you are, Father," Martin said, and his voice too gave the impression of carefully imposed restraint. His eyes strayed to Edith's door and then back to his father. "Conference in the hall?"

"Mr. Sands and I are talking," Andrew said.

Martin raised his brows. "Not by any chance about me? You're looking very guilty."

"Guilty?" Andrew laughed, but one of his hands crept up towards his face as if to smooth away the lines of guilt. "It's difficult for you to believe, Martin, but people frequently talk about other things than you."

"Granted."

"I . . . Polly is not here. She's gone down to meet Lieutenant Frome. I expect they'll be married this afternoon."

Martin flicked another glance toward Edith's door. "Nice day for it."

"My suggestion entirely," Sands said.

"Don't bother with explanations," Andrew told him curtly, and turned back to Martin. "I want you to go down there now — where is it? — the Ford Hotel?"

"Yes."

"Go down there now. I — well, I forgot to give Polly some money. I'll write a check and you can take it down to her and — and wish her luck. Wish her luck for me, Martin."

"This is a damn funny time to ask me to go traipsing around with checks and touching messages."

"I'm not asking you, I'm telling you. Come downstairs and I'll write the check."

He went to the staircase, and after a moment's hesitation Martin followed him, frowning at Sands as he passed him. If Sands had not been there he would have made an issue of it and insisted on an explanation from his father. But Sands was there and in some strange way allied with Andrew, and together the two men had a personal ascendancy that Martin would not defy.

Besides, he was a sophisticated young man and dared not show surprise. In the study he accepted the check from Andrew docilely, but with a quirk of his mouth to show that he was not in any way impressed.

"Wish her luck," Andrew said again.

"Sure," Martin said, and departed with a debonair wave of his hand.

The sophisticate, Sands thought, the man about town, the babe swaddled by Brooks Brothers.

"Sit down and make yourself comfortable, Mr. Sands," Andrew said. "We have quite a lot to talk about. Cigarette?"

"Thanks."

"Do you mind if I close this door?"

"Not at all."

"I wouldn't want the maids to hear me talking about my murders. It might destroy their faith in doctors." He closed the door. "Murders, I don't know how many, or how many causes . . . Faulty diagnosis, too much pressure on the scalpel, bad timing, sheer ignorance and lack of experience. . . . Every time I lost a case I used to brood about it. Then I began to believe that some time between now and the end of time everything would be put right again. In the forever-ever land the dead baby lifted by Caesarean section would have its second chance, would breathe again, and live, and grow beautiful. Mildred called it *having faith.*"

The smoke from his cigarette slid up his face. "You used the phrase, humanly impossible. Practically nothing is that. A man can endure anything if he believes in ultimate justice, if he believes that somewhere dangling in space is justice and the wicked shall be punished and the good shall be rewarded. That is the working principle of the religion of the people I know. Revenge and reward."

He leaned forward. "Think of it! Somewhere dangling in space justice, great impartial justicc built likc a monstrous man straddling the universe. A big fellow, a strong fellow, a kind fellow, but still like us, with sixteen bones in each wrist and his pubic hair modestly covered with a bit of cloth."

Sands thought, another fallen idealist, the man who expects too much and loses his faith not all at once but gradually and with suspense and bitter doubts.

"Don't be boyish," he said, and glanced at his watch. "My friends will be here in five minutes."

"And then?"

"And then," Sands said carefully, "I will try to prove that you are a murderer."

"You have no proof?"

"Circumstantial evidence only. Quite a bit of it in Greeley's case. You had the means of committing the murder and you were around at the crucial time."

"So were a lot of other people."

"True. Then Miss Green's death offers no problem to you. You can only be charged there with moral guilt, moral irresponsibility. Evil and fear grow like cancer cells, inexorably, aimlessly, destroying whatever they touch. Cora Green was one of its victims." He blinked his eyes, dreamily. "Circumstantial evidence only," he repeated. "Perhaps we'll have to wait for that big fellow straddling the universe to get you."

"I'm not afraid of him."

"What?" Sands said in an exaggerated drawl. "And him so big and full of vitamins?"

They both smiled but there was a glint of rage in Andrew's eyes and he crushed out his cigarette with a gesture that was almost savage.

"You are making me out a fool and a villain. I am neither. I am an ordinary man, and if out-of-the-ordinary things occurred to me, they occurred naturally. You understand? They just *happened.* You said it yourself. I was not looking for that diary when I found it, I had forgotten there was such a thing. I was looking for the scarf Lucille gave me last Christmas, a black scarf with little gray designs on it."

"Black? With little gray designs? It sounds terribly cute."

He leaned back, watching Andrew lazily as if the whole episode was a mildly amusing joke.

A flush of anger rose slowly up Andrew's face. He knew that Sands was baiting him, that he must control himself. But he felt too that he must impress the man and make him realize that he was not a child to be laughed aside.

"The scarf was not in the cedar closet where Lucille said it was. I looked in my own room and then in hers. The diary was in one of her bureau drawers. It wasn't even hidden properly, it was just there. As if she took it out now and then to read . . ." He stopped, sucking in his breath. "Think of it! She murdered my wife. And all these years she's kept the evidence to convict her, casually, in a bureau drawer."

"It may not have been there all the time," Sands said. "Perhaps she'd hidden it well, and came across it and wanted to read it again." Why? To re-live it, and by reliving it to lay the ghost that haunted her mind?

"I think you're right. She'd been thinking of Mildred that day, Sunday. Martin and I found the sketches she made of Mildred.

She had burned out the eyes with a cigarette." He paused again, shaking his head half in sorrow, half in bewildered rage. "The systematic illogic of women. A man cannot believe it. When they are angry they are cold and merciless. When they have a grievance they tuck it up their sleeve and it comes out at some inexplicable and unconnected moment as tears. They can live, almost happily, with a man they hate, and harry a man they love to death."

"Like yourself?"

"Like myself, yes. All my life I've been fair prey for any woman, because I value peace. I gave up my independence for the sake of peace. I've hired myself out to a series of managers — my mother, Edith, Lucille. A man has no redress against the soft lilting command, no refuge at all from the voices of the women who love him and are doing everything 'for his own good.' "

He was no longer angry. He even seemed bored with his own words, as if he had said them to himself a great many times and was now reciting a piece of memory work.

"I killed Edith," he said.

Sands did not reply.

"I killed her because she started to nag at me. She wanted a sleeping prescription, so I gave her one. I hadn't planned anything, hadn't thought of it. But suddenly there she was, wanting to be put to sleep. You understand? It was so simple, so predestined. She asked for it."

"Yes."

"I went in after she was dead, to find the diary and destroy it. But it wasn't there. I didn't worry about it, however."

"You should. It might help to hang you."

"No, it won't. This talk is confidential between the two of us. And the evidence against Edith is too strong. Your friends will find morphine in Edith's glass, and I will supply the letter she wrote to Lucille at Penwood."

"Edith was the only one who couldn't possibly have sent the amputated finger to Lucille."

"You can't fool me like that," Andrew said. "You will have to bring me to trial one case at a time. You can't try to prove that *perhaps* I killed Greeley, and *perhaps* I killed Edith, and have the two *perhaps's* make a certainty."

"That's right."

"Why do you want to hang me, anyway? Revenge? Punishment? To teach me a lesson or teach other people a lesson?"

"It's my job," Sands said wryly.

"Purely impersonal?"

"No, not quite."

"Why, then?"

"I think you might do it again."

"That's ridiculous," Andrew said. "I have no reason to kill anyone else."

"Perhaps you had no reason to kill Greeley?"

"He was interfering, getting in my way. I hadn't planned on killing him or anyone else. I hadn't really planned anything. I was pretty dazed after reading the diary, I hardly remember driving out to meet Giles. All I could think of was Lucille's two faces — the one she showed to me and the one I saw in Mildred's diary. I thought I would keep quiet until after Polly was married and then I would confront Lucille with the diary. But what then? Would she confess? Would she lie? Would she even try to kill me perhaps, to save herself? Then we came upon the train wreck and the situation solved itself. I knew how I could test Lucille. I saw the finger in a slop pail and I picked it up and wrapped it in my handkerchief."

The grotesque picture formed in Sands' mind. The man bending furtively over a slop pail, wrapping the finger carefully in his handkerchief, like a jewel.

"You know how it makes you feel when

you do something like that?" Andrew said. "It makes you feel a little crazy."

"It would."

"It was only a test for her, you understand. I had to know whether she was guilty. I didn't foresee the actual results — it wasn't even her own guilt that drove her crazy, it was the knowledge that someone else *knew* of her guilt, and was pointing it out, that someone had tracked her down. She, who had lived a placid, happy life for sixteen years now found herself a criminal." He paused. "I keep thinking of what she did when she opened the box. She screamed we know that, and then she must have run to the bureau drawer to find the diary. When she saw it was gone, she knew one of us must have taken it."

"A pretty symbol, that finger."

Andrew shrugged away the implications.

"I carried it in my pocket for the rest of the night. In the morning I bought a box in the dime store on my way to the office, and wrapped it. I thought of sending it through the mail, but then I saw this shabby-looking little man standing beside the newsstand. I asked him if he'd deliver a parcel for two dollars and he said he would."

"You could have saved yourself trouble by lowering it to fifty cents. A parcel worth a two-dollar delivery is worth opening. Childish of you."

"I — it just didn't occur to me not to trust him. I've had no experience with such things."

"The first thing he did, of course, was take it to a washroom and open it. Maybe he was a little surprised by it, but I don't think so. Greeley had seen a lot of things in his life. What interested him was the smell of money, and he got a big whiff when he opened that parcel. He delivered it, all right. Then he waited around to see what would happen. He followed Lucille down to Sunnyside and waited outside while she was in the beauty parlor. When she came out he confronted her. She gave him a fifty-dollar bill to keep him quiet. She took a room at the Lakeside Hotel, and when he was pretty sure she was going to stay there for a while he went out and had what for Greeley was a big evening. Life was all right for Greeley that night. He had champagne, even if it was in a third-rate joint; he had a girl, no matter how many other people had had her; he danced, though his legs must have hurt him; he had a shot of morphine for a cheap dream, but most of all he had a future.

"Lucille must have promised him more money, for he told the girl he was with that he had a date, and then he returned to the Lakeside. He got there about the same time as Inspector Bascombe and I did. Men like Greeley have a sharp nose for two things — money and cops, and he probably recognized us right away. He didn't know what we were there for. Maybe it was Lucille, maybe not. He hung around the alley for a while, and then you came along. He recognized you immediately."

"It was a shock," Andrew said, "it was a terrible shock to me to meet him again. I'd almost forgotten about him. Then I saw what I should have seen the preceding afternoon if I hadn't been intent on my plan — he was a morphine addict. I could see his eyes clearly in the light of the hotel sign, they were pupil-less, blind-looking. The tragedy of it was that I was carrying my instrument bag in case I'd have to give Lucille a sedative."

"Tragedy?"

"He saw I was a doctor."

"I see."

"Yes, a doctor means only one thing to an addict — a chance for more dope. We're all pestered by them at one time or another. The first thing the man said was, 'A sawbones, eh?' I told him I wasn't, but he didn't believe me. He seemed to be burning up with triumph. I could see then what I had let myself in for. I had committed no crime, but I had done what most people would consider a revolting thing — and I wanted it kept secret. But Greeley, you understand, thought I *had* committed a crime.

" 'Some parcel,' he said. 'Where's the rest of the guy?' I didn't answer him. Then he asked me for some morphine. He told me he had a hard time getting any and what he did get was diluted. 'I haven't got any extra,' I told him. 'Just a quarter grain, not enough for you.'

"The crazy part of it is that if I hadn't refused to give it to him at first, he would have been suspicious. But because I refused, he said, 'What do *you* know about me? That'll do — for *now.*'

"He didn't need it then, he was pretty full of the stuff already. But he couldn't pass up the chance, you see. They all have that same senseless greed because they know what it's like to be without it. Anyway he led me around to the alley. It was dark and intensely cold. I put my bag on the ground and opened it. Greeley lit a match and cupped it in his hands, and then we both squatted down beside the bag. Bizarre, isn't it, and somehow obscene?

"I could tell you it was then that I decided

to kill him, but I couldn't tell you why. There was no one reason, perhaps there never is for a murder. Perhaps I killed him because I was afraid of him, and because he hadn't long to live and would be better off dead anyway, and because he had betrayed my trust, and because of the very ugliness of the scene itself.

"It was no trick to kill him. He had no way of knowing how much I was giving him. Besides, he kept watching the end of the alley and urging me to hurry up. I prepared the syringe and told him to take off his coat. He said, 'What the hell, nothing fancy for me,' and shoved out his arm.

"I gave him two grains. The whole incident didn't take ten minutes."

Two grains, ten minutes, the end of Greeley, Sands thought.

"Simple," he said. "Natural. Practically an accident."

"I told you that."

"Sure. Any logical sequence of events ends in murder just as the logical sequel to life is death."

"Irony doesn't affect me," Andrew said. "I was trying to present my story sincerely and honestly. I feel that you are a civilized man and can understand it."

"It's easy enough to be civilized in a

vacuum. The mouse in an airless bell jar can't be compared to ordinary mice. In the first place he's dead."

"Quite so."

The doorbell began to ring.

"Your friends are here," Andrew said politely.

While the policemen were there Andrew remained in his study with the door shut. Overhead, the men worked very quietly, and only by straining his ears could he hear them moving about.

What are they doing up there?

Nothing. Don't listen.

What have I overlooked?

Nothing. It is all arranged. Poor Edith killed herself in remorse.

Poor Edith, how like Greeley she'd acted after all, both so greedy for a little death and so surprised at getting the real thing.

He didn't worry about either of them. About Greeley he had no feelings at all, and while he felt sorry for Edith because she had made her own death necessary, he did not wish her back. He had turned a corner in his life. Looking back he could see only the sharp gray angle of a nameless building, and ahead of him the road was a nebula of mist swirling with forms and shapes, faces that were not yet faces, sounds that were not yet sounds. As he walked along the mist would clear. But right now it was frightening. It stung his eyes and muffled his ears and curled down deep into his lungs and made him cough. He could taste it in his mouth, fresh like the snow he had eaten when he was a child.

I don't feel very well.

Andrew dear, have you been eating Snow?

I don't feel very well.

The child is Ill. Call the doctor Immediately.

Calling Dr. Morrow. Calling Dr. Morrow. Dr. Morrow is wanted in . . .

Andrew my Dear. Snow is full of Germs. It may look pretty but it is not to Eat because it is full of Germs. I'll buy you a microscope for your birthday so you can see for Yourself how many Germs there are Everywhere.

Many many many many Germs. Everywhere.

He became aware, suddenly, that the noises overhead had ceased. The house was empty. Mildred had gone, with the children, Edith was gone, and Lucille — only the maids were left and they must go too. He had to be alone, to think.

He rose painfully. His legs were cramped, he had been sitting too tensely. He must learn not to look back or look ahead. Where, then, could you look? At yourself. Turn your eyes in, like two little dentist's mirrors, until you saw yourself larger than life, in great detail, each single hair, each pore of skin a new revelation, wondrously crawling with germs.

But the silence, the appalling silence of the man in the mirrors; the brittle limbs, the face mobile but cold like glass . . .

He crossed the hall, quickly, to escape his own image.

He found the maids in the kitchen. They had been quarreling. Della's eyes were swollen from weeping and Annie's mouth had a set stubborn look. She didn't change her expression when she saw Andrew.

"I say we're leaving," she said. "I say there's too much going on around this place that don't look right."

"Of course," Andrew said. "If you feel like that."

"She don't want to go. Afraid she won't get another job. Why, in times like these they get down on their knees and beg you to take a job. She's too dumb to see that."

"It's different with you!" Della cried. "I got to send money home every month!"

"Don't I got to live too! And am I scared?"

"I'll give you both a month's wages," Andrew said quietly. "You may leave today if you like."

Della only wept harder, and Annie had to do the talking for both of them. It was real kind of Dr. Morrow, really generous. Not that they couldn't use the money. Not that they *wanted* to leave him in the lurch like this. But what future was there in housework?

"What future indeed?" Andrew said. "You may leave at once. I'll make out your checks."

They went upstairs and began to pack.

"Remember the emeralds?" Della said wistfully.

"What emeralds?"

"You remember. The parcel."

"Oh, hell," Annie said and jerked open the closet door savagely. "We're too old to play games like that. You're eighteen and you talk like you were ten. Imagine us with an emerald."

"Maybe — some day we'll find something. Money or something. Or maybe radium. They say if you find just a little bit of radium you get to be a millionaire."

"Will you shut up?" Annie banged her fist against a suitcase. "Will — you — shut — up?"

They hadn't many clothes to pack. Within half an hour they were on Bloor Street waiting for a streetcar, their purses tight beneath their arms. They were still quarreling, but there was a softer look on Annie's face and now and then she scanned the sidewalk and the gutter. Just in case.

Andrew stood at the door, watching, long after they were out of sight. They were gone, the last remnants of the old life, and now he must begin his new one. But he felt curiously tired, reluctant to move from the door, as if any movement at all might bring on a new situation, a new series of complications that he would have to deal with. He wanted to see and hear nothing, to feel nothing, to be alone in a vacuum, like the mouse in the bell jar.

But the mouse was dead. *In the first place he's dead.*

He heard someone coming down the stairs behind him. He had thought the house was empty, but now that he found it wasn't, he was too weary to feel surprise. He turned slowly, knowing before he turned that it was Sands.

"I thought you were gone." He had to drag the words out of his mouth.

"I'm leaving in a minute. Everyone else has gone. You'll be alone."

Alone. The word had a solemn sonorous sound that struck his ears with a thud.

"That's what you wanted," Sands said. "Isn't it?"

"Yes."

"Well, now you have it. You'll be alone. And you'll be lonely."

"No, no, I — Martin — Martin will come back."

"But he won't stay. There's nothing left for him here in this house."

"He'll stay if I ask him to, if I . . ."

"No, I don't think so. You'll be quite alone."

Andrew closed his eyes. He saw the mist on the road ahead suddenly sweeping back toward him in gusts of fury.

"No — no . . ." he said, but how faint and suffocated his voice was, with the mist smothering his mouth. "I'm not — not afraid of being alone."

"You're afraid of the big fellow. You don't want justice any more, you want mercy."

Andrew bowed his head. Mercy. A terrible and piteous word that conjured up all the lost people wailing to their lost gods.

"I want nothing," he said.

"But it's too late now. You already have what you wanted. Don't you recognize it?"

Sands smiled. "This is *it,* Morrow."

"Is this it?" He heard in his own voice the wailing of the lost men.

"The role of avenger is not for a little man like you. You dispensed justice to Lucille, now you must await it, in turn. You even asked the police to help you hunt her down. You couldn't wait, could you? . . . You enjoyed seeing her suffer, didn't you?"

"No — no — I'm sorry . . ."

"Too late, it's all over."

"And now?"

"Now, nothing." He smiled again. "Doesn't that amuse you? You're like Lucille, after all. You have nothing left to live for."

Andrew was propped up against the wall like a dummy waiting for someone to come along and move it into a new position.

Sands took out his watch, and in the silent house the ticking seemed extraordinarily important.

He put his watch back and began buttoning his overcoat. "I've got to leave now."

"I am afraid," Andrew said, but the door had already opened and closed again, softly, and he knew he must die alone.

Sands stepped out into the keen sparkling air.

He stood on the veranda for a moment

and looked across the park where the phallic points of the pines were thrust toward the sun. He felt outside time, naked and frail and percipient. Evergreens and men were growing toward decay. Time was a mole moving under the roads of the city and imperceptibly buckling the asphalt. Time passed over his head in a thin gray rack of scudding clouds, as if the sky had fled away and its last remaining rags were blowing over the edge of the world.

The employees of Thorndike Press hope you have enjoyed this Large Print book. All our Large Print titles are designed for easy reading, and all our books are made to last. Other Thorndike Press Large Print books are available at your library, through selected bookstores, or directly from us.

For information about titles, please call:

(800) 257-5157
To share your comments, please write:

Publisher
Thorndike Press
P.O. Box 159
Thorndike, Maine 04986